A Circle of Shadows

By: Zosha Durano

It began with Queen Hildegard's executive order.

It cited the mysterious killings that appeared to have been occurring over the past month. She said her administration believed it to be a new pack of savage beasts that migrated from out of nowhere. She said that neither the curfew nor the increased number of guards were working to abate these vicious attacks. She said the only option now was to have every single citizen of Orienne report to the castle, where they would be protected until more was learned.

There had indeed been killings, without any signs or warnings—nothing except faint screeches that could be dismissed as casual background noise. The bodies of villagers would be found sprawled across the street, slashed so brutally there was hardly anything left of them. At least that was what the word on the street was.

And so, every villager reported to the castle: every nobleperson, baker, blacksmith, tailor, criminal, family.

The guards had them sign in, and then led the women down one hall, the men the other, and the children another. As the women were ushered away from their families, the guards told them it was for organizational purposes, that the separation would not last.

They did not search for those who did not show up as ordered, but that night all the women heard the screeches. And they were not faint background noises but loud bloodcurdling shrieks.

There was a commotion as the outside doors started pounding, the walls almost shaking.

The next day, the guards had them cough over every single one of their belongings and clothing, switching them out for monotonous dresses and assuring them they would give them all the food and supplies they needed when necessary. They explained they had to conserve resources and keep track of everyone.

The women were not allowed outside, for obvious reasons as the beasts were out there. They were also not allowed to wander any farther than the west wing corridor, which consisted of nothing but empty rooms and hallways. Guards were posted to make sure of this and escorted them to the room where they would eat and the giant room where they would sleep.

When the women wondered why the elderly and sick were being taken away, questioned the restrictions, or said they wished to see their families, the guards explained it was for the sake of safety precautions as mandated by Queen Hildegard.

When more time passed with nothing to fill their time with and even less answers, the women pushed, and the guards pushed back, locking a few of them into small closets until they calmed down. They said they were doing it for their own good. Those who fought back too hard received a couple blunt blows, and were thus brought to the sick ward where the elderly and ill were brought. No one ever returned from there.

One day, after the guards had herded the women into the bed space, the head guard spoke up, saying an announcement was to be made: there had been an invasion by the creatures on the other side of the castle, and all the men and children had been wiped out. Other than Queen Hildegard, who was safely tucked away in her own hidden and confidential corner, only they remained. The gasps and wails that filled the room could split the castle in half, before the head guard called for silence and order.

Time passed. The castle deteriorated. The food supply had started off thin and the quality poor, but it came even smaller and worse as time wore on.

Every once in a while, at night, they would hear the bloodcurdling shrieks outside. And the guards would remind them how lucky they were to be safe and away from all of that. How grateful they should be, with a flock of vigilant angels always on their shoulders.

Amabel thinks this room used to be the trophy room. I've always leaned more towards armory. It's large enough to fit several series of weapons and armor. There are also no windows and no hints of mirrors ever being here, which could just be a good show of cleanliness, but I think demonstrates there truly never were any. And if so, this helps my case—mirrors are not needed for armories; a knight need only take his supplies and leave. But why have a trophy room with no vessel upon which to gloat at you and your treasure?

Either way, it is nothing but a semi-large, worn-down room now, just like how the rest of this place might as well have started off as a dark warehouse, for the five years of poor upkeep has left it with no resemblance of the grand castle it once stood proudly as.

But I remember.

"That looks revolting," the woman a couple heads in front of me in line grumbles to herself.

"What did you say?" the guard handing us food says.

The woman tenses, struck by horror. "Nothing, madam."

"If this serving does not please you, you are welcome to wait until tomorrow's meal for something that does."

"Not at all! It looks delicious."

"Carry on."

"Please, madam! I-I'm starving!"

"We *all* are," the guard retorts.

"What's this?" the head guard, Commander Ingrith, approaches. Everyone in line stiffens, turning away like they would melt into the floor if they could. The entire room quiets down, though no one dares to watch or even look this way. I avert my eyes as well, as much as it pains me—but only because I can't afford not to.

"It's nothing, madam," the woman quickly and desperately says.

"It seemed for a moment you were disrespecting the grace bestowed upon you. After all we do to gather it."

"No, never!"

Ingrith backhands her, and she tumbles to the floor. A couple guards come over with the flick of her fingers. They take turns stomping on her, as she cries in agony. Ingrith lifts her hand up, making them cease. "You take care to remember what we do for you here. Don't ever address any of us like that again." She and the other guards leave her on the floor.

The women closest to her start to bend down with their arms out, but before they can reach her, she slips away and hurries to an open seat, crying softly.

We all do our best to brush all this off as if it never happened. That's the only way to make it here.

I glance around as I carry my plate of food away, surrounded by other women walking back to their tables. Everyone slowly returns to their conversations and food as we all try to ignore the collective uneasiness draped over the entire room. I think through my options and calculate the logistics of each one. Having figured it out, I angle my plate ever so slightly so a roll of bread tumbles onto the floor as I pass that woman. I keep walking, pretending not to notice and not daring to look back. No one else seems to notice either, but I hear a very tiny excited gasp.

I bring my plate of food over to the wooden table in the corner of the room, the spot next to Amabel, my best friend, left vacant for me even if I am the last one at the table of six. Right now, Colette and Odysa are sitting with their backs to me, and they murmur something to each other. "Etta," Odysa says before they both move in for a kiss. They are such a lovely couple and they know it.

I sit next to Amabel, her pale face acting like the glow of the moon in a place where the sky is absent. They all get silent as I sit, and I know by now it is not out of fear or discomfort but respect. The guards here do not appreciate the fine nuances between such atmospheres, and they are all too content to breathe in that murky air of supposed superiority—but not I. Respect is a power and a gift that is earned, and I am privileged to have earned theirs.

Nonetheless, tension weighs heavily over our table.

"She seems like she's going to be alright," I tell them quietly.

Odysa just stiffens further. I set a hand on her shoulder. "Let your worries ease," I say gently, and she exhales slowly.

I stare at the food before me, a small pile of circular, moist chunks. "Anyone care for a second helping of beans?" I ask the table.

"Sure," Amabel takes me up on my offer. I scrape the squishy lumps off of my plate and onto hers. "You know, you keep disrupting my healthy streak. What kind of friend are you?"

I smile, grateful for any source of levity.

Colette also chuckles. She has golden-brown skin, round hazel eyes that make her seem even more young and doe-like, and dark brown hair. Her pocket wiggles.

"It decided to take a trip today?" I ask.

The mouse pokes its head above her pocket, the ends of its whiskers bending against the worn fabric of her dress. "He must have realized he would get more food if he came along now rather than visited me later," she says. Anyone who hasn't had more than one conversation with her would think she was talking quietly, before realizing that that is just her regular volume of speech; she is merely a soft-spoken individual. She glances to make sure the nearest guard is a good enough distance away and not looking before she drops a bean into her pocket.

I also steal a couple quick glances, making sure to be subtle about it, solemnity taking over our table. "Tomorrow," I say under my breath.

Odysa's brows twitch. "Even after Ingrith's little display of affection?" she whispers.

"That's merely Ingrith being Ingrith. It changes nothing. If anything, it's all the more reason to." I reiterate firmly, "Tomorrow," those at the table nodding in agreement and hushed conviction.

I look at the table next to ours. "Do you think we'll have beans again tomorrow?"

The same graveness stirs through them, a couple of their eyes twitching before control is quickly regained. Ravinn shrugs and says, "I suppose so. It's become such a staple, that by now I do not even want anything else."

I turn to the table on the other side of us, Lella making eye contact with me, a serious gleam passing between the two of us. "I was just speaking to them about our food, and they believe tomorrow will present the same course. What of you?"

Her table exchanges glances, a quiet fire rolling through them. "I know not, but I look forward to whatever food tomorrow brings." I offer her a smile before turning back to those at my own table.

"Are we certain this is the best strategy?" Odysa whispers.

Just then, a flurry of violent screeches and cries sound from outside. Only a couple women from other tables flinch; for the most part we are all used to it by now. It goes on for several minutes like thunderclaps of a tormented sky and it does not truly end but merely gets quieter. It just switches to become part of our landscape, a dark cloud hanging over our heads.

"That," Ingrith booms, "is what you are all being protected from!" She targets random women to stare down, not leaving them until they cower and avert their eyes. She of course picks Odysa, as if expecting a new outcome from her, but she just glares right on back like always. I extend my leg under the table, lightly knocking her good leg. Instinctively, Odysa turns towards me, and this is enough to break their excessively intense stare-on.

But then Ingrith's eyes land on me, either inadvertently or pseudo-inadvertently. I tilt my head down very slightly, a small gesture of understanding of my place, but I don't forget the flashing twitch of my lips into a half-smile—the one that makes even her solid, tight cheeks soften into a blush she hurries to shake off. Sure enough, her marching pace quickens past us, but not before she sends me a warning glare.

It's such a fast and subtle exchange that no one else would ever notice, except for Amabel because she knows me too well and I keep no secrets from her. She chuckles softly.

I return to Odysa. "Anyway, you were saying?" I challenge her.

"I still think we should consider trying our luck out there. And if Orienne's too ravaged and broken, we can make a go for it somewhere else. Make our own kingdom, or maybe discover an existing one along the way."

Orienne has always existed by itself, as its own world. In all this time, there had been cartographers, but they only ever found out bits and pieces of information about other civilizations—mostly the fact that any that existed were much too far to bother with. They're just arbitrarily named now, after each explorer that claims they exist.

"The strongest and most equipped explorers couldn't wander far enough to find solid evidence of other kingdoms. I've told you before, we don't have time and resources to bother with this—not while Orienne is overrun by monsters that will strike us down the moment we step outside," I whisper.

"How do we know there even *are* any monsters out there? We've only ever heard them, but never seen them with our own two eyes."

"*Something* killed my brother five years ago." I had heard that sound, the one they talk about, the one that's just like an irksome ringing in your ears, before the crushing shriek took over and I saw his broken body.

"But how do we know it was the monsters? How do we know anything Ingrith and the rest of her cronies ever told us has any basis in reality?"

"We cannot be certain either way. It's best to deal with the devil you know."

"And what's your plan in the instance that this fails?" Odysa says. "We can only have the element of surprise once."

I look at her lame leg, her crutches leaning against the edge of the table. "And how do you plan on surviving out there in your state?"

She tenses up, Colette glancing at her as if to assess what is going through her mind and if she needs to step in.

"Yvette," Amabel scolds me quietly.

But I had to put it in perspective. It would be cruel to not show Odysa the reality of the situation before letting her wander head-first into it. I would much rather be harsh than cruel—especially when it comes to the people sitting at this table.

Odysa replies, "I would rather die at the hands of a wild animal than remain a prisoner."

"Perhaps neither has to occur," I say firmly.

Odysa gives in, sighing reluctantly. "I hope you're right, Yvette."

***

Ingrith leads all of us back to our sleeping quarters where the hundreds of beds are organized. She seems to make a point to not look at me.

I head over to my cot, which is right next to Amabel.

Everyone else who is in on the plan has their cot in the corner, as planned, to have them perfectly positioned, switching with others when necessary. This was all done months and months ago and at scattered points in time, so the guards wouldn't notice or if they did would have forgotten by now.

As I lie there, I stare at the ceiling high above that is rusting, worlds away. I wonder how many flakes of paint fall down from the ceiling and land on us without us knowing, how many times pieces of this other world collide with our mortal bodies.

I roll my eyes at myself. Mutinies really do make you feel existential, I suppose.

The guards wander along the narrow aisles separating the cots. Though narrow, the aisles have gotten much wider as time went on. I hope Ingrith didn't think we wouldn't notice it.

But if I'm honest, it seems that many of the other women here never did. Or at least pretended not to.

There were a lot of protests against how things were run very early on, but they numbed out. It's as if most people forgot or simply no longer cared. They just accepted this new world as theirs.

But that's the last thing I wish to do.

I rotate my body towards Amabel. "Do you remember when we would perform here?" I whisper.

She smiles, her brows twitching a little like she's surprised I'm bringing it up now of all times. "Yes. Me with my lute, you with your voice." Her face falls. "Lucine with her flute."

Lucine had been one of the women who demanded truth, cooperation, and looser restrictions in the beginning of all this. Not long after, she was summoned out of the dining hall during dinner and never seen again.

We quickly learned to stop asking questions and creating fusses. Not like that, at least. Anything we did had to be cunning and calculated.

"Do you remember the first time we got an invite from Queen Hildegard?" I say, trying to not let the sweetness of the memory die out.

It seems to work for Amabel beams. "We could hardly believe it. Of course, the castle was nothing new to you, but me—I almost lost it."

"It was still my first time performing here. But yes, I remember you nearly stained your dress."

Amabel almost fails to stifle a burst of giggles, and I smile fondly. We became regulars after then, performing for nearly every occasion Queen Hildegard hosted in her grand ballroom—which is now our sleeping corridors.

I scoot closer to the edge of my bed, and hum softly, so that it is barely above a rumbling vibration in the back of my throat. Amabel strums her fingers against an imaginary lute on her bed, swishing her head about lightly.

I halt abruptly as I go back to watching the guards. Many of them start making their way out after a minute or so has passed of them scanning every cot, presumably to go to their own quarters for rest. As always, they leave no more than two on each of the four far corners of the room and Ingrith at the mouth of the door, the only exit and entrance from here. From what I've observed and confirmed, there are also a couple other guards posted on the ends of the hallway outside—but far enough away that they are not a big concern for the logistics of my plan.

Ingrith and I lock eyes again for a brief moment. I curl the very ends of my lips up in the most daring and inviting manner, the tip of my eyebrow flashing up just very briefly. Like before, it's quick enough that anyone else would miss it, unless they are concentrating on no one but me. Unless a part of them is seeking that brief hint of a look.

Ingrith shoots me a glare that sharply twists her gaze at me as if to say 'Who do you think you are? You really thought, huh?"

I secretly smirk at her weak attempt of a cover-up. I glance back at Amabel. The bricks are being laid.

Then, with the last of the extra and now unneeded guards walking past her out the door, Ingrith follows them out, a clunky *click* sounding as she locks us in from the outside.

***

We wake up to the dull clanging of the bell.

We gather ourselves and follow the guards out of the ballroom. I steal a backwards glance at Ingrith, the last one out. Just like every single day for the past five years, she takes out the ring of keys always dangling on the hook of her belt and rotates it so the largest key, a silver one that is crooked at a most particular angle, is pointed and fitted into the lock.

I don't know why they wake us up and force us out of the ballroom, only to have us wander idly for the next couple of hours until it's lunchtime. Recently, Amabel and I began volunteering to clean the walls and floors out of desperation for anything to fill this boredom. A couple others joined us—they must have been just as bored out of their minds as we were. Considering we cannot go anywhere without asking permission and being escorted, we're not allowed any personal possessions, and there is absolutely nothing else to do; boredom is like oxygen here.

Besides, the monotony allows me to capture every detail of the world before me.

As I dunk the washcloth into our communal pail of water and soap and scrub the crackled stone pillar, I hear the rhythmic clacking of Odysa's crutches against the stone floor, Colette beside her, having come from the library (not the actual royal library; this is a much smaller room with a much smaller supply). Even if she now reads every single day, my heart still beams proudly every time I see her holding a book or coming from doing so. I just can't help but think back to when I first offered to teach her, and how skilled she has become since those four years ago.

"Watch it," Ingrith snaps at Odysa.

"Pardon?" she says, the aggression clear in her voice.

"Your crutch nearly grazed my foot."

"It was nowhere near you, and even if it was, that would be your fault for sticking it out in front of a pedestrian. Goodness, how did you become commander, being so thick?"

I cringe.

Ingrith raises the back of her palm as if to strike her, halting a hairbreadth away from her face. Colette instinctively clutches Odysa's arm, ready to yank her out of harm's way. But Odysa hasn't flinched in the slightest, and even now she merely stares at Ingrith with a raised brow. Ingrith shakes her head at her. "Don't expect lunch. Queen Hildegard is not offering her precious supplies for the likes of such ungrateful insubordinates such as yourself."

"Oh, that really hurt me," Odysa says mockingly, moving away.

Damn it, Odysa, not every vex is a battle to be fought!

She catches sight of my displeased eyes—and pretends not to.

You'd think that on the morn of our plan, she'd at least practice some restraint.

Out of the corner of my eye, I spot a tall, plump woman with black hair walk pass a stout lady with angular eyes and a small round nose, just barely brushing against her side, never slowing down for a moment.

I sigh, leaving the pillar, sticking my washcloth into my pocket, and speed-walking into the midst of all this. "Rowena!"

The tall woman spins around. "Oh, why, hello, Yvette! Whatever do I owe the pleasure?"

The woman she walked past glances from her to me, utterly puzzled.

"I know what you did; now return it." I look at the woman, a vague image crawling into my mind from scattered words I'd heard from Odysa about her. I lean in closer so she can very clearly read my lips and my face and I speak slowly. "Your name is Freya, correct?" She nods. "She stole from you," I say, pointing at Rowena, then Freya, then Freya's pocket.

Freya pats her pocket, feeling its vacancy and turning back to Rowena in disbelief.

"Why am I the culprit? How do we know this isn't a case of clumsiness and mindless minds?"

Freya looks extremely uncomfortable, like she just wants this whole ordeal to end, no matter how it does so. Rowena really chose to pick the easiest target. "Just hand it over, already."

"Is everything alright?" a guard leans in and asks. She is even taller than Rowena, and has dark brown skin and curly hair that sticks out from her helmet.

Freya tenses, despite being the most innocent one of the three of us. She bobs her head sporadically.

"Are you certain?" the guard asks. Her eyes are soft, and her question is straight and clear, appearing to be a genuine one that is not layered with ulterior motives. But there's only so much you can decipher from a three-word sentence. And there's only so much trust you can grant someone in a position of power such as hers.

I give Rowena a look. "Of course," she says, pulling out a needle and a tiny spool of red thread that only has one line left in it from her pocket and returning them to her. "Freya was just showing me what she got."

"I just happened to find it, Dame Anice, and Commander Ingrith said I could keep it," Freya hurries to explain through her muddled voice and thick lisp.

"I know," Anice says, smiling and patting her shoulder. "Well, let's carry on then, shall we?" Freya steals a glance at Rowena and me before scurrying away. The guard—Anice—examines Rowena and me one last time before leaving us be.

"Spoil-sport. It's a dog-eat-dog world, you know," Rowena says.

"What would you do with it, anyway?"

"More than her, that's for certain."

A thought crosses my mind, and not for the first time. Imagine what an asset it would be to have someone as sneaky and stealthy as Rowena on our side. She would be so much better than me at swiping important objects; I can get it done with effort and meticulous forethought, but she can do it in her sleep. And the more pieces that can be assured and set in stone, the taller and sturdier we can stand.

"Rowena, do you ever miss your old life?" I ask carefully.

She shrugs. "I always say there's no use dwelling in the past."

"What if I'm speaking of the future?"

Rowena scoffs and shakes her head, amused. "I always knew there was a keen fire in you," she says, then her smile smooths into a straight line, "but I make a point not to get entangled in other people, thank you very much."

Well, there's that.

She walks off.

"Rowena," I call her one last time. She turns around, tired of me. I put my hand out. She does not even attempt to put on an act this time and just slaps the washcloth back in my hand.

I have to assume that was just a practical joke fueled by pettiness because what else would she do with a dirty washcloth? I head back beside Amabel. She gives me a sympathetically annoyed head shake. *This is what we have to deal with*, it says.

I roll my eyes in agreement. *They really know how to pick their moments.*

"Yvette," a soft voice behind me says, hardly louder than the sound of our washcloths rubbing against the pillar. I turn to see Colette, standing patiently.

"Hello, Colette."

She glances at the pillar. I hand her an extra washcloth and she leans in closer to join us in cleaning. "I saw you talking to the guard, along with Rowena."

"It's nothing to be worried about. She was just trying to con someone," I assure her.

She nods, knowing that is something Rowena would do.

"Are you alright?" I ask her. She is too good at hiding her emotions, but I can sense something off-balance within.

"I'm a little scared," she whispers, and her voice is only steady from the rest of her working overtime.

I think about what's going to happen tonight. The riskiest play we could make, one that we've been building up for months and that will put not only our friends' lives on the line, but the lives of every single woman in this castle. Everything is going to change, and if it isn't in the precise manner we are hoping for, it will all be for naught and we will all be doomed.

"Good," I reply. "That makes me feel better about being a *lot* scared." I nudge her with my elbow.

She lets a smile fall onto her face.

"What were you reading in the library?"

"History."

My heart glows. There's only one history book in that library. The one I arbitrarily yanked off the shelf a couple years ago and sounded each word out to Colette over and over until she could do the same to me. "Were you feeling sentimental?"

"Never."

We chuckle.

"People who read history willingly are a mystery to me," Amabel chimes in disapprovingly. She puts a hand up before either Colette or I can interject. "And no, there is no amount of emotional value in any specific volume that can make it more interesting."

"That's because you just don't like reading," I point out.

She shrugs. "Why open a book when you can have infinitely more fun cleaning the same couple of pillars for hours on end?" I push her lightly, and Colette laughs quietly.

"I'll leave you two to your fun, then," Colette teases, standing up. I catch Odysa peeking at us from the corner, where Colette goes to meet her now. When our eyes meet, she smiles awkwardly, more a straight line than anything. She clearly knows I am less than happy with her right now.

But if Colette of all people is feeling jittery enough about everything to admit it out loud to me, I imagine Odysa must be, too.

Fine. I'll be the bigger person for this instance. But she owes me for next time.

I let a smile through, and with this invitation Odysa curves her lips into a real smile, albeit still sheepish and begrudging.

"I hope you know how much they look up to you," Amabel tells me, resting her washcloth in place against the pillar. "How much we all do."

"I do. And I don't carry it lightly." I have a promise for every single one of my friends, these dear women, imprinted in my soul. I won't let them down. I will guide them, I will protect them, and I will take care of them in all the ways they expect me to and in all the ways I can.

***

I should feel more uneasy, or at least some indication of understanding the gravity of what is moments away from unfolding. But as we are all escorted back into the ballroom in two long, straight lines, I don't feel an inkling of any sort of graveness. I just know what I have to do.

Once everyone is in bed and the guards start making their rounds, I exchange glances with Amabel, and I make my way to Ingrith.

Her body stiffens but her eyes soften, a strange paradox that only she can pull off.

"Pardon me, madam," I say.

"What?" she snaps.

"I know this is past our wandering hours, but I was wondering if you would permit me to go to the privy."

"You had your chance earlier. Why did you not make use of it then?"

"I did, madam. But you see, I am in need once again. Silly how our bodies always seem to beg something from us. We can plan ahead, use our brains to steer them away, but we cannot stop the bodily needs, the physical sensations, that run through and take control of our being."

I examine her upturned and observant eyes, her narrow and poised lips, the faint wrinkles crinkling from the edges of her eyes. I drop my voice to a husky whisper. "And when we try to push them aside, they just find their way back up to the surface. You understand?"

She shakes herself out of her daze. "No one is permitted to leave the sleeping corridors once it is lights' out. Unfortunately for you, it is now lights' out."

I step closer to her, invading her personal space. "You would be there, guarding me with your valiant sword. Watching me with your all-knowing eyes. Protecting me with your fearless, commanding spirit. Keeping me from any form of harm. All in the name of our Queen."

"The rules are the rules, peasant."

"Perhaps you can make an exception."

"Why in the world would I afford you such a thing?"

"Because I'll make it worth your while."

"Whatever do you mean?"

"Oh, Commander Ingrith," I say, letting her name roll off my tongue like a steady stream of water over pebbles. "You have been the head guard for all these years, always working, never resting." I've captured her eyes with mine and they are wound tightly. "I think you deserve a bit of rest, even for just a moment." I snatch the keys off the hook on her belt and her sword from its sheath, in one fell swoop.

The weight of the sword surprises me and drops my arm down before I strain it back up again to point at her. Meanwhile, Amabel and Ravinn have leapt out of bed and are already shoving the giant doors shut, and the others have already charged at each of the two guards in their designated corners. Colette has already hopped on the back of one, wringing her elbow around her neck and her legs around her abdomen and hips, while Odysa swings her crutches against the guard's face. They all gang up on the clearly outnumbered guards, kicking and punching and holding them back once they get the chance to.

Ingrith looks at me, not shocked nor worried, just furious and waiting to see my next move. I am about to throw the set of keys at Amabel, but then I realize something that fills me up from my toes to the roots of my hair with cold dread—the key to the ballroom is not here.

"Keys!" Amabel shouts, her arm stretched out.

The key I've seen Ingrith use countless times to lock the ballroom is not here. The key to our entire plan is not here.

Ingrith watches on.

"They're not here!"

"What?!"

I can hear the squeak and rapid impact of running footsteps outside, coming closer. How are they already so close?

I leave Ingrith and rush towards the nearest empty cot and shove it towards the door. Amabel leaves Ravinn, who is pressing her back against the giant pair of doors, to help me move it, and we almost make it. But the doors start popping open, crack by crack, and Ravinn does her best to force it back shut, but it's quickly too much to handle and she is flung to the side as dozens of guards come flooding in.

This is not how this was supposed to happen.

I whirl my sword into the first guard that comes in; her armor absorbs most of the blow but it still makes her stumble back.

I look back at the other mutineers, my friends and comrades. They had managed to tie up or knock out the guards stationed at each corner, as I knew they would, but I have no idea how any of us will be able to take on this new storm. Still, they run towards the new guards, and they all collide in the aisles between the beds.

All those not involved hop from their beds and run to the far corners, their hands in the air.

Rosy, who sat beside Ravinn at the table next to mine and who I often found cleaning beside me, gets stabbed and falls straight to the floor, her eyes frozen in an eternal gaze. All I can do is gawk. No one was supposed to die.

Colette trips a guard from behind. She slams what looks like a broken chunk of her bedframe against the guard's head as she goes down, cracking the guard's head, and then snaps her neck with one sharp twist.

As I duck a jab, I realize Colette knows what has to be done. We can no longer lock everyone in and take hostages until our demands are met and negotiations are settled. We must go for the kill in order to somehow weasel our way back on top, or at the very least *out* of this. I charge forward, the guard before me parrying.

I hear a groan, one that rises above all the other noises, not because it is loud but because it has a twang of home in it. I turn to see Amabel doubled over, a sword through her body. The guard pulls the sword out, her pale face colorless as she clatters to the floor. Years of a beautiful human life, and she is disposed of so carelessly.

There are bodies all around. My friends are getting killed.

Everything is falling apart.

Those still alive see the bodies as well and it paralyzes them like it paralyzes me. In the corner, I spot Colette gasping, her body jerking up and down in heavy hyperventilating gasps, before she passes out. Odysa grabs her arms and drags her away to the side, away from all the chaos.

In the midst of all this, I had forgotten that I was in the center of my own duel, and the sword in my hand is suddenly no longer there. I must have gotten disarmed without me noticing. The guard's face is triumphant. I look down and see the blade that is impaled through me. She yanks the sword out and this time I feel every jagged inch of the blade's path through my body. It debilitates me and I collapse onto the floor.

Ingrith bends down before me. She grabs the nape of my neck and brings my head up, rotating it to scan around the room. To see the number of bodies. There are only about three of my friends left, out of the 18 that we started with, and they are bruised and bloodied and surrounded by the guards. They look at me with utter defeat.

In my peripheral view, I see Odysa and Colette off in a corner with those who were not involved. Ingrith doesn't turn my head towards them, and she does not point them out.

It seems they may have gotten lost in all the hullabaloo. Besides, who would suspect someone like little, soft-spoken Colette, or Odysa with her crutches, to partake in such daring and vicious an act as this?

Odysa holds Colette's unconscious body tightly, staring into my eyes, the words written as clearly in them as if she were saying them out loud. Words of guilt, apology, grief.

I do not dare let my eyes stay on hers any longer than that passing glimpse so as to not create any form of suspicion for who will be our only escapees. I hope she caught the assurance I tried to send her before I tore them away so quickly.

"You were right," Ingrith says. "You did make this worth my while."

Tears fill my eyes.

This cannot be.

I still have plans, so many plans.

I was going to gather all those with literacy skills or knowledge of some sort of trade and to institute an education system.

I was going to turn each room into its own specific shop so that the castle would be transformed into something more like a village.

I was going to establish a voting system that would afford every single woman the opportunity to have a say in each matter of this castle.

I was going to slowly build trust and harmony between the guards and the villagers, and eventually gather a group of brave souls to explore the rest of the castle—whether that ended with collecting the decomposed bodies of our brothers and children or reuniting with them would be a later issue but one that would finally be resolved.

I was going to change things, and they were going to be good changes.

No one even knew I had these plans, for I figured I would have so much time and there was no need to pile these stressors upon my friends while we were still figuring out how to get there. And now…

I spot Rowena, in the corner with the rest of the innocent, uninvolved women, her hands also in the air.

Oh, how could I have been so stupid!

Chapter Two: Rowena

"See, now, this is why order is of such essence!" Commander Ingrith's voice echoes in the large room. "For years, we have done our best in such trying times to keep everyone safe and well. Queen Hildegard desired the well-being of as many Oriennan citizens as possible. But I have also been ordered to ensure the longevity of Orienne, and that was threatened tonight. There are enough dangers to be protected from, and any additional threats to your livelihood cannot be allowed."

"Get these bodies out of here," Ingrith commands, and her guards get right to it.

I look at Yvette's corpse. Her hooked nose, thick eyebrows, long black hair like the rolling tides at nightfall, skin like lush wheat. She had a different kind of gravity about her, a way of just pulling you in.

Believe me, I do not feel guilty at all—she got herself into this mess and dragged her friends down with her. And I have my own matters to worry about, my own self to take care of—but still. It is quite a shame she had to die unnecessarily.

One of the guards pulls her up, strings her body over her shoulder, and brings her out of here.

Dame Anice comes in with the cleaning pail.

"You three," Ingrith points at the three mutineers. "I want no hint that any of this ever happened. The good women here deserve a painless area for rest."

The guards keep their weapons pointed at them as they slowly soak the rags into the bucket and scrub into the thick, sticky blood. One begins to sob uncontrollably, halting to catch her breath.

"I said no hint," Ingrith barks.

But she doesn't stop sobbing, even as she cups her mouth tightly. She tries to go back to her task, but then she vomits.

"Clean that as well," Ingrith orders.

She wipes her mouth with the back of her sleeve, taking a couple deep breaths as the other two stroke her. She goes back to cleaning, but not before glaring at Ingrith.

But this seems to mean nothing to Ingrith; why should it, anyway?

I see Freya a couple people over. She looks just as pained as the mutineers are, like she might become sick to her stomach.

Please, she hardly even knew them!

I feel a set of eyes on me. Heavy as boulders and as scalding as fire. They are Odysa's. I scowl at her, silently saying 'What do you want?' I glance at Colette, who she is cradling tightly. She must have gotten hit with another one of her fainting spells in the midst of all this. Goodness, she really ought to keep away from Odysa.

Finally, Ingrith becomes satisfied with the three women's cleaning. "That's enough." She gestures at the guards watching them and has them follow her out of here. Nearly all the others stay inside here, several covering every section of the room. She pulls out the ballroom key from the inner breast pocket of her armor as she walks out, and I hear the clunky click as she locks us in.

***

The next day after they wake us up, they offer us the choice of one of three fruits. I suppose they wanted to give us a bit of a pick-me-up after scarring most of the others for life with a live massacre last night.

Colette is near the front of the line, and it is almost her turn to select from the three baskets laid on the table and watched by the guards. She has her head turned down, her hair falling over the sides of her face.

I squeeze behind her, inciting a groan from the woman behind me that I cut, but with the sharp stink-eye I send her she silences.

"Hello, hello little Etta. Which fruit will you getta?"

"The apple," she replies curtly. The guard hands it to her, and she nods a "Thank you."

"You have the choice between an apple, orange, and pear, and you go for the apple?"

"Why not?"

"Child, you need someone else to make your life decisions for you." I snatch an extra pear from the edge of the basket before the guards notice and slip it into her open hand.

32

"Let it be yours," she says quietly as we move away from the guards.

I pull out the three fruits I already took, hidden in the upper torso of my dress—one of each. "Choosing is just so difficult, you see."

She tries to move past me, but I stand in her path. "At least give it to your rat."

"That mouse does not rely on me for any of his needs. The relationship is one of mutual respect, not ownership and dependence."

"Alright, Pied Piper. I didn't realize one fruit would crumble your entire ecosystem."

She pushes the pear into my hand. "I seek no favors from you. And only Odysa calls me Etta."

She moves around me, leaving a huge gap of space between the two of us. She meets Odysa, who is sitting against the wall in the middle of the hallway. She plops down beside her and gives her the apple.

"Rowena." I turn to see Anice approaching. "Commander Ingrith summons you."

I thought she would. I follow her down a couple passageways. She opens the door to a cellar, where Commander Ingrith is standing inside. I go in, Dame Anice closing the door and standing outside.

"You're welcome," I start off.

"Pardon?"

"For yesterday. I assume that is why you brought me here."

"You think too highly of yourself, peasant. You're no more than a snively crook that happens to have a tendency for being in the right place at the right time."

"Now, now, I may not be as honorable as you, but I wouldn't reduce myself to so low a regard. For something to occur at such a high tendency as it does for me, there has to be more at play than luck, and you know it. That's why *you* always come to *me*." I add, "Madam."

"I won't dispute your value, but I do not wish to overinflate your sense of importance."

"Consider it deflated, then. And if I find out anything more, I will let you know, but it seems you have gotten everything under control." I hesitate. "I must say, however, I was rather surprised you let the events yesterday unfold rather than nip them right in the bud."

"Are you questioning my authority?"

"No. I was merely expecting you to arrest Yvette and Amabel right away, as is usually done, before all that bloodshed."

"I wanted to know every single person who was involved. Thankfully, I let it be, for it was much larger than you let on, and now we appear to have everyone in their rightful places."

A thought stirs in my mind, but I stomp it out of existence. "It appears so. Well done, madam. Are we off to the ward now?"

She purses her lips. "It's rather sweet how your mother is the only thing that can warm your cold heart."

I chuckle dryly. "Yes, the only thing."

"A mother's love works mysterious wonders no other force is capable of. But about her…"

I tense up. That is not a good start to a sentence.

"She is just so old, you understand."

I instantly catch on. "Are there not enough people already? You have the three mutineers now, as well."

"Look, her age would be acceptable, her blindness would be acceptable, even her occasional delusionality would be acceptable—if it were not for her sickliness. She is falling ill nearly every other month, and is taking up far too many of our very limited resources. We can no longer afford to keep her here."

"Why not simply allow her to pass?"

"You know why."

"Madam. I have offered you so much inside information and pointed you in the correct direction time and time again for years. Orienne would not be standing before me as it is—*you* would not be standing before me as you are—if not for me."

Innocent, ignorant Yvette must have believed wholeheartedly she was the first one to revolt. She *was* the one that went the farthest, but there were many other scattered whispers before her that spelled revolution. However, they all got squashed before they could culminate into anything bigger since *I* heard or saw something of suspicion and slipped it along to Ingrith. And for her to disregard all that now…

"I appreciate all you've done, but there reaches a point where I must weigh your aid against your long-term request. For a long time, the scale has been at a balance but alas it has now tipped to the opposite side."

"Madam—"

"I will allow you to bid a final farewell."

She leads me out of the cellar, my head still stuffed with too much to sort through that I just feel disconnected from the rest of myself. Anice trails behind us, setting a hand on my shoulder. I stare at it until she awkwardly drops it.

We walk past other wandering villagers and stationed guards, the privy coming up. "May I be pardoned for a moment?"

Ingrith nods, and the two of them stand outside it as I go in. There are a couple seats inside with small holes upon which to do your business over. It is a dim and dingy room, as most rooms here are.

I feel the prickling in the back of my eyes, the twisting torment in the pit of my stomach. I bite my tongue, forcing it all back down.

I check again just to make sure I truly am alone. Then, I pick at the corner of a loose brick on the wall, wiggling it out. I unfold the corners of the makeshift wrap I created to reveal my pile of vials, foods, and other little trinkets I've collected over the years. I stick the fruits in here.

Then, I reach deep inside this hole and grab the small purple vial in the very back. I hold it up, squinting at the couple of drops of liquid in the limited light, then stuff it into my pocket. I cover up all the items in here again and place the brick back over it.

When I head back out, Ingrith leads me down hallway upon hallway, each one getting emptier as we move on. We make it to the very edge of the west wing corridor, where no one else is permitted to go, and she nods at the couple of guards posted. By now, they are used to seeing me.

We cross an empty hallway that always seemed like it should be haunted and likely is. I hear muffled groans and cries in the broom cupboard we pass. This is nothing new; I would be surprised if I *didn't* hear anything.

In the middle of this hallway is a rickety wooden door with a single guard in front of it. Inside is the sick ward: a lounge of cots and a couple tables, no more than about a dozen people occupying it. It's one of the few rooms I've been in with a window, and the only one with a series of them along the wall. But they are all barred up. Coughs and sneezes fill the air like background music, and those who aren't sick are grey.

My mother is seated at one of the tables, peeling her orange with their shaky hands.

Commander Ingrith extends her hand in a 'go-ahead' gesture and I approach her, she and Dame Anice standing in place by the door. Before I even sit before her, her head turns in my direction. "Rowena?"

"Yes."

She finishes peeling her orange. "Would you like some?"

"Sure."

She tears off just a single piece and holds it out for me.

"Thanks, Mother," I say with an edge of sarcasm.

"I need the vitamins more than you, silly." She coughs.

"Fine, fine, I believe you," I say.

She chuckles.

"What have you been doing to occupy yourself in recent days?"

"Oh, the usual. Talking, walking—come hither." She stands up slowly, holding the edges of her chair to push herself up. She pats around until she grabs my hand and drags me across the room, using her other hand to hold onto the edges of tables and walls to both support her strides and guide her vision.

She leads me to a free space against the wall, standing in front of a window. She feels the window sill. "Can you feel the air? It's colder here."

"It sure is." You can't see much of the outside from here, just the weed-ridden courtyard, and a slice of a corner of the village, which is nothing more than a bunch of abandoned, run-down houses and buildings.

"But it's covered with bars. Beware, Rowena, for they only put bars in a prison."

She brings me back to the table, leaning on my arm for support now.

"You know, I was playing cards with another person here and she was so shocked at how I was able to do so without seeing," she says.

"I don't even know how you do it."

Mother laughs. "People assume that because I'm blind or old, I can't do anything. Someone tried to take my food from me—you best know I grabbed her wrist and made her apologize to me." She looks around, then points to the side. "That's her on the other table; I recognize her distinct scent."

The woman cringes. She is a relatively young woman with copper brown hair and freckles. She coughs into her hand. "I apologize, I meant no—"

I narrow my eyes at her warningly and she shrinks away.

"Worry not, she will not do it again. Now, have you met a man yet?"

I barely say "no" before she starts rambling, "Igor is a good man. The blacksmith's apprentice. Easy on the eyes and easier on the heart. We're getting married, you know."

I sigh. "It will be a beautiful ceremony."

"He's slippery with his love, though. Slippery." She starts coughing, muffling it with a tissue. "You know, I worry about Rowena sometimes. She has two doting parents but she still loses her way."

I hold both of her hands. "There's no need to worry about her. She takes care of herself just fine."

A very distinct sadness takes over my soul, drowning me. I take a good look at my mother. She has a hunched back and does not move with as much agility as she once did, but the rhythm in her motions is steady and strong. She is frail, but not fragile. She is not completely lucid, but she is vibrant.

"I'm going to hug you," I tell her.

"Well, alright, then."

I get up, bend down before her, and embrace her, soaking in that sweet spot of tightness that is right below the level that triggers the aching in her back. She rubs my back and pats my shoulder, but it is more a polite gesture than one that truly screams what I wish it did. And it is not because she doesn't want to, but because she just doesn't quite remember.

I hold her a little longer before letting her go. I pat her arm with one hand, pouring the entire contents of the vial into her goblet, making sure my body covers it up from Anice and Ingrith's angle.

"Take care now," I tell her, shuffling away hurriedly.

"Off so soon?" I hear her say, not quite realizing I'd already left.

I nod at Ingrith and Anice and follow them out, not looking back once.

***

They leave me alone once they have led me back to the general population, not saying another word.

I lean against the wall, crossing my arms, so many different things bubbling up inside me. I want to punch the wall. Knock that pillar down. Beat the first person that crosses me to a pulp.

I need to find Colette.

I march through the hallways, not caring if I bump into other women, peeking inside any open rooms. Alas, I spot a little, doe-eyed woman inside the library. Thankfully, I don't see Odysa anywhere.

It can barely be called a library, considering how small the room is and how meager the book supply is. The door is ajar with about three other women inside, flipping through the books, a guard posted beside the door.

"May I enter?" I ask the guard. She nods and I head in.

Colette glances up, sighing with frustration when she catches sight of me. She moves to the third bookshelf, the last shelf there is, on the far end of the room.

I walk briskly towards her, encroaching on her space. Now that I'm this close to her, I see the dark bruise above her eyebrow that is mostly covered by her hair. "Stay away from Odysa," I growl.

She barely looks up from her book, not expending energy on me. "Why?"

"Because she's no good for you."

"You realize it will never happen between you and me."

My mouth drops and my face twists with disgust. "Ew, no! You could not be farther from what this is all about!" I shudder, and then wave my hand dismissively. "Just stay away from her, understand?"

She flicks her eyebrow up, shrugging with that instead of her shoulders, dismissing me without a thought.

I stretch my sleeve up and push out the shard of glass I keep tucked into it at all times. I inconspicuously jab it against her rib, just enough for her to feel pressure but not enough to slit through her dress.

She finally looks at me, but nothing on her face has changed to anything besides indifference. "You'd kill me over so petty a matter?"

"I once bled a man dry just for insulting me."

I recall it—I was walking through the streets at night, trying to get home after a long day. I passed through a quieter street, where there was no one but me and the silhouette of a middle-aged man that strayed behind me. His silhouette became a body as he got closer and closer to me, whistling at me as if to reduce me into nothing more than an animal for him to make his own. He cornered me, trapping me with his arms. My hands shook as I reached for the knife hidden in my dress and slit his throat.

They stopped shaking as I watched my would-be assailant crumple to the ground before me.

I never once lost a moment of sleep over it.

"I'm familiar with the rumors," Colette says, still not the slightest bit fazed.

"Then you understand how serious I can be."

"Sure," she says, going back to her book.

I press the shard harder against her before releasing her and slipping it back in my sleeve. She continues reading.

Furious, I go to slap the book from her hand; she slides it away just in time, barely even trying. My jaw twitches. Goodness, I could strangle her. Instead, I march out of here, knocking a couple books off the shelves as I pass one of the other women.

The guard peeks inside and locks eyes with the woman. "Pick those up," she berates her.

***

I spend the next hour or couple of hours—time blurs together—sitting against the wall, just staring. Staring at the people who walk past me. Staring at the worn stone pillar. Staring at the floor.

A pair of feet position themselves before me. Their owner squats before me—that deaf woman. What's her name? Freya?

"What do you want?" I say, not looking up, desiring nothing more than to be left alone for the rest of eternity.

She doesn't reply, just keeps her eyes on me, like she's waiting for me to meet her gaze. Then it hits me—of course she needs me to meet her gaze. How else would she read my lips?

"What... do... you... want?" I repeat.

"Any sort of wound cleaner," she says—too loudly for my liking.

"Shush!" I snap, flinging a finger over my lips and looking around to see if anyone heard. She winces. No one seems to have taken notice. "What do you need it for?" She opens her mouth and I wave my hands. "Actually, no." She closes her mouth again and watches me closely. "What makes you think *I* have anything like that? Sidonie is the one who actually apprenticed her doctor father." I point at her from across the hallway.

Freya shrugs timidly.

I think for a moment, glance around, then lean in. "I have a bottle. Reduces swelling, pain, blood, infection." I find myself inadvertently using gestures for each word I say. Her eyes light up. "You can use it on a couple of conditions."

She nods fervently.

"I want your lunches for the rest of the month." It's not like I need to store extra food, but who knows when it could come in handy—that's my motto for everything I come across.

"Done."

"And I need to be there when you use it. So I can monitor how much of it you use."

She bites her lip.

"Both conditions, or no medicine. And I'll still find out what it's for."

She puts a hand out. "Deal."

I leave her hand in the air and stand up. "Wait here."

I walk behind ambling women, enter groups of walkers, slip past pillars and corridors in the most nonchalant ways possible, and finally sneak into the privy without calling the attention of a single guard. Someone else is in there this time, so I force myself to actually use it as well until she leaves. Then, I wiggle the brick out. I slip the vial from earlier back in its rightful place and switch it out for the translucent, slightly bigger but still objectively tiny medicine bottle.

I sneak back to where I left Freya, who is still standing there like a patient schoolgirl. I jerk my head to the side. "Guide my next move."

She brings me to a quiet corner in a hallway that is less bustling. The nearest guard is the one at the very end of the hallway. Odysa is slumped against the wall. She straightens up and tenses when she sees me. "What is she doing here?" she complains rudely, making different gestures for each word she says.

"That's no way to greet someone bearing gifts." I pull the medicine just high enough above my pocket for them to see it before I shove it back in.

Freya eyes me and looks back at Odysa, conveying the necessity. Odysa sighs. "Fine."

I hand Freya the bottle and we both kneel down beside Odysa. Freya gets very close to her, angling herself so the majority of her body blocks Odysa's in a way that none of the passersby can sneak a look. But I make sure to squeeze in just enough that *I* have a good view.

Odysa rolls up her dress to expose an ugly cut on the upper thigh of her lame leg. There's a rip in her dress right above it, but it is so thin that it can be overlooked. The only thing that gives it away is the fresh, red lining.

I make a tight "O" with my lips. "Where did that come from?"

She looks at me, annoyed.

"Nail," Freya explains. "Came loose in her bed frame and scraped her in her sleep."

"Sounds like the frame needs some fixing."

"It's taken care of, but your concern is flattering," Odysa says sourly, still moving her hands about in that language of hers and Freya's.

Freya pats Odysa's arm before she pours the medicine directly over her cut. Odysa obviously has no reaction, for she cannot feel a thing. "That's enough," I say, gripping Freya's elbow and she stops abruptly.

"Why isn't Colette here?" I ask.

"You have a knack for sticking your nose in businesses that aren't yours," Odysa snaps.

"You have a knack for refusing to answer simple questions of curiosity."

Odysa rolls her eyes. "If you must know for *some* reason, I did not inform Colette so as not to worry her over something as minor as this. I wasn't even going to do anything about it myself if I didn't run into Freya and she hadn't made such a fuss."

"I see." I set my hand out for Freya to place the medicine bottle in. But she doesn't.

She puts a finger up. "One more."

I raise my eyebrows. "Pardon?"

Odysa pulls the collar of her dress down to reveal her shoulder, where there is a smaller but equally ugly cut.

"And that's also from your bed frame?"

"It's a thin, old bed and I'm an active sleeper."

I groan and cross my arms. She's already used about ten percent of the bottle. I'm about to watch her use up another ten percent.

Freya pulls Odysa's collar further down, soft smiles exchanged between the two of them. She pats her shoulder, the dim gleam of her silver ring and the little, worn lace around her wrist catching my eye. A fresh zigzagged line of red thread connects what would otherwise be a tear in the middle of it. "What's that?" I point it out.

"Surprise—it's another matter that's none of your concern!" Odysa exclaims.

I raise an eyebrow and eye the medicine bottle in Freya's hand, a subtle threat to revoke the deal.

"It's alright," Freya assures a not-so-certain Odysa. "It's the matching ribbon my daughter and I used to always wear together." She smiles wistfully, a longing gripping her tightly. Odysa looks at her closely, her chest swelling like she is about to say something, but she eyes me and lets the moment go by wordless. Freya pours the medicine over this wound, and this time Odysa hisses through her teeth. She lets out a shaky, prolonged exhale as a couple women casually pass us.

Alas, Freya finishes up, pressing ripped parts of her dress against the wounds until they stick. She hands me back the medicine.

"Pleasure," I tell Freya. "Rest easy," I tell Odysa and she scowls at me.

"Bug off," she grumbles.

I put my hands in the air in offense. "Relax, I was merely pulling your leg."

Her hands clench up. "Inebriate scum," she growls at my back as I walk away, chuckling at myself.

At a distance, I turn and look back at them, peeking between other wandering women at them. Odysa squeezes Freya's hand. Then she leans in and mutters something to her. She repeats it a couple times, but I am too far and blocked to get a good line of sight and I miss it each time. Freya shakes her head at Odysa, as if in disbelief and absurdity.

I think about this whole exchange, mentally underlining it, not sure when it will come in handy but storing it for when it does.

***

That night, the screeches are louder and more pungent than ever. They start in the middle of dinner and persist into our sleeping hours.

"Remember, all," Commander Ingrith booms, "it is a privilege and a gift to be here in our warm arms rather than out there at their cold mercy."

I turn to my side, pulling my blanket tighter around me. It takes a little longer tonight, but eventually the monsters' cries turn into white noise, a cold lullaby from the back of their tone-deaf throats that forces me into sleep.

***

"Rowena," Ingrith calls me back as I follow the trail of women out of the sleeping corridor the next morning.

"Good morning, madam," I say dryly.

She sticks the key into the door of the sleeping corridor, but when she twists it, it gets jammed. Her jaw twitches as she yanks it back out and retries, locking it successfully only the second time.

"Do you have anything you wish to tell me?" she says.

"I could use a couple days before I find something else of substance. I'm not exactly an information dispenser, madam."

"Watch your tongue, peasant." She points her finger at me threateningly. She grabs my arm and pulls me even farther from everyone else, even though we are already out of earshot. "Your mother was already lifeless when my guards came to collect her."

49

I gape at her. "Was she, now?"

"Any idea how that might have occurred?"

"Well, she had a bit of a cough, but I did not realize it was that serious. She always found her way back, no matter what circumstances ransacked her health. I suppose you just never truly know."

"Enough of this!" Ingrith whispers so sharply she could slice me in half. "From the looks of it, she was poisoned."

My eyes widen.

"Where did you obtain it from?"

I shake my head. "I didn't—"

She backhands me so hard I wobble and crash against the wall.

I rub my cheek. "I—"

She backhands my other cheek, making me side-step in the other direction now.

"Commander—"

She grips my neck with her cold, gloved hand. "Do not waste my time."

"Madam, if I dare say so," I croak, "why does it even matter? Either way, she's dead."

She releases me, and I take in deep breaths, rubbing my neck. But now she grips my elbow and drags me along with her. This catches the interest of more than a few people, both guards and villagers, but when she turns her stone-cold eyes upon any of the spectators, they whirl around as quickly as if they never saw a thing.

She leads me into the dead land that is past the west wing corridor and stops before the broom cupboard. It's silent today.

Dame Anice is guarding it this time, and with a nod from Ingrith, she pulls out the only key she seems to have possession of and uses it to unlock and open the door.

Odysa is in here, too, leaning against the far corner of the cellar.

Ingrith tosses me inside, and I almost land on Odysa but she moves away in time for me to just crash into the vacant shelf on the wall, making it wobble.

She glowers at me, her eyes transforming into wolf fangs that rip me apart into shreds. It dawns on me—she thinks I tipped Ingrith off about her.

I could shake my head, or send some sort of subtle message that I had nothing to do with this, but I don't. I will let her think what she thinks. Even if it's not true this time, it would have been true another time. Hence, it makes no difference now.

Ingrith stomps inside, only needing to take a couple steps to be up close to Odysa and me, given how the cellar only allows for a limited number of steps in every direction. "I want the truth, the entire truth, out of both of you before I leave this cellar."

"How could I have any part in what occurred the other night? I can barely even walk, let alone participate in an ambush!" Odysa protests.

"That's never stopped you from being disruptive to me or my people every opportunity you got," Ingrith snaps.

"Well, that stopped me this time," she argues.

Ingrith looks so angry she could explode, and her body seems to rise up like she is about to. But then something passes over her and she soothes back down. She leans back, crossing her arms haughtily. "How have you been feeling lately? Has your health been faring well? For you seem more tired and burdened than usual. Perhaps you ought to pay a visit to the sick ward."

Odysa tenses up. Not from discomfort but preparation. She might not know what I do, but everyone is well aware of the fact that no one returns from there. "That does not scare me."

Ingrith examines her from head to toe. "Fine, then how about that little one?" My stomach twists into a knot. "What's her name? Colette? You seem to spend a lot of time with her. She has that sleeping condition, does she not? Perhaps *she* should be transferred to the sick ward."

Odysa's eyes widen, horror and fury blazing in them. "Don't—"

"I got the poison from Freya," I chime in.

Odysa gawks at me.

"Is that so?" Ingrith says, interest piqued.

"She may not be any sort of doctor but she has a way with medicines—Odysa, you can attest to this—so I asked her if she had anything of the like, and she coughed it over with no strings attached, the kind soul that she is," I say. "I wouldn't be surprised if she has other secrets lying about. As I mentioned before, I did see her conversing with Yvette on the day of the revolt."

"I see," Ingrith says, turning around to reach for the door.

"That's a lie!" Odysa cries. "Freya doesn't have any possessions on her, let alone dangerous ones! And you've seen how she only ever keeps to herself! This conniving snake is grasping at straws. Don't you dare fall for—"

Ingrith slips outside, the door locking a moment after.

Odysa is silent, panting heavily at the door.

Then, she slams her body against me, crashing me against the wall, her crutches clattering to the floor. She leans her arms against me, pinning me.

I scoff at her. "Is this supposed to intimidate me?"

Apparently, she has other plans, for she starts pounding her fists against my face in rapid motion, one right after the other. It takes me by surprise to say the least, and it takes me a moment to recuperate and shove her down to the floor.

My face is ringing from the series of bruises she just indented into me. I rub the blood off from underneath my nostrils and I slam my foot into her stomach, making her fold in half. I swing my foot back to send her another kick, but this time she grabs hold of it as it meets her and she flings it, sending me toppling down next to her.

She uses her elbows to crawl on top of me, picking up where she left off with the pounding. I shield my face as much as I can with my elbows, letting her punch them instead. I twist my arm to face her, and her next blow lands right on top of where I keep the glass shard fastened. We yelp quietly in unison, the glass cutting both of us simultaneously. But I don't mind that I'm bleeding there now, so long as she is as well.

The door unlocks, and Dame Anice peeks her head in through the narrow crack. She takes in the scene before her. "Settle down, you two. Don't make this any worse for yourselves."

"It's already gotten worse!" Odysa retorts. "How can you stand there, letting Ingrith do this? How can you take part in all this?"

"You are the ones stirring the pot needlessly."

"Oh, for crying out loud! You have to know that none of this is just."

"I..." She silences, closing the door abruptly. A couple seconds later, the door opens all the way, and Ingrith is there, gripping a blanched and cowering Freya.

Odysa hoists herself off of me, leaning against the wall to slowly bring herself up, and grabs her crutches again. I rise to my feet as well, brushing myself off.

Ingrith shoves Freya in, and Odysa releases one of her crutches to wrap an arm around her, warmly and protectively.

"I'll give you a couple minutes to reflect on the current situation and gather your thoughts. By the time I return, there better be an answer that pleases me. Depending on the degree to which it satisfies me, one of you may get off scot-free." She glares at each one of us, the threat reaching down to our souls before she leaves once again.

"Odysa," Freya says, her voice even more distorted as tears choke it up.

Odysa holds her shoulder. "It will be alright," she says, moving her hands about in that systematic way that only she and Freya know of.

I roll my eyes.

Odysa looks around the bare cellar. She glances at the shelf, which seems to have shifted at an angle slightly off from where it is meant to be from me getting thrown against it. I didn't notice before, but there's a very small slice of light coming from behind it.

She uses her crutches to get closer to it and peeks behind. There's a window there. She calls Freya over with a jerk of her head, and the two of them go on either side of the shelf, slowly heaving it slightly above the floor and pushing it, very quietly moving it so there is enough space to move behind it.

The window has thick metal bars striped over it vertically. Odysa holds one and rattles it. It wobbles, rickety and loose in her hand. Freya's eyes widen, the fear and excitement evident in her. I watch with interest.

Odysa shakes it a little more and it pops off, making the window hum with the vibration. Freya gasps quietly. I glance at the door and back at them, biting my lip nervously.

There are four bars left. Odysa and Freya take hold of the next one, shaking it together. This one is not as loose and puts up more of a fight with battle cries in the form of light creaks. I cringe. "Hey," I grumble at them.

The doorhandle rattles. Odysa stuffs the broken bar in the skirt of her dress and pushes Freya to the other side of the cellar, opposite of the window. She stands in front of it, perfectly obscuring the missing bar on the window.

Ingrith comes in. "Well?" she says, eyes bouncing over each of us.

Freya puts her hands in the air innocently. Odysa says, "Nothing other than what has already been laid before you."

Ingrith observes the shelf and narrows her eyes at Odysa. She approaches her, snatching her arm and pulling her away from the wall, revealing the window. The broken bar clatters from inside her dress and lands between her feet. Ingrith's jaw twitches and she yanks her sword out, pressing it against Odysa's neck. Freya lets out a squeaky cry.

"I was only trying to look out the window and the bar fell off," Odysa says, eyes squeezed shut, with a sort of fear I had never seen in her before. "I swear to you."

"She speaks the truth," Freya sputters.

Ingrith turns her piercing eyes onto me. "And what is your say in all this?"

Odysa peeks her eyes open to look at me, defeat already spelled out in them as she braces for the end.

"She saw the light poking out and moved the shelf back to investigate it," I say.

Ingrith listens, waiting for me to get to the good part. Waiting for me to handfeed her the most delicious delicacies. Waiting for me to wipe the drool off her chin that drizzles down from her ravenous jaws, jaws she always keeps on display, even if it makes her mouth ache, just for the hopes of making us cower.

"When she moved the shelf away from the window, the bar popped out on its own," I decide on a whim. A flash of surprise goes through both Freya's and Odysa's eyes before they quickly stifle it down. "It appears the shelf was the only thing keeping it up."

Ingrith's eyes harden over mine, like a cold and hard realization is sinking into her. I try not to gulp and keep my own eyes steady on her, terrified yet satisfied with knowing this can serve as the 'not today' that I want it to and the 'damn you' that she deserves.

She releases her sword from Odysa's neck and swishes it over me several times. They are quick and large slices that dash across the entire width of my body and overlap with one another like a child's scribbles over a wall in their home.

I stumble back, reaching for something to hold onto to balance myself, but I find nothing and drop down.

Odysa's jaw drops. She charges at Ingrith from behind, clawing at her face. Ingrith quickly manages to get ahold of her and elbows her face. "Anice!" she calls, and Anice slithers in.

Ingrith binds Odysa's hands behind her, and Anice ties Freya up in the same way. They tie Freya's legs and Odysa's good leg to the shelf, so tightly they are essentially stuck in place. Ingrith kicks Odysa's crutches, and they slide past me to the opposite end of the cellar, hitting the wall with a soft impact.

Ingrith examines me. She leans in close, and at first, I think she is going to say something to me, but she just rolls my sleeve down and takes away the glass shard. She throws her head back at me one more time with a glint of disgust and disappointment, and Anice just averts her eyes as they both leave once more.

"Rowena?" Freya calls, her voice wavering.

I swallow sharply. They are both watching me, which should be a good thing. After all, I'd hate to be bleeding out on the floor and just be ignored. But I hate the pity beaming off of them.

"They're going to feed you to them, you know," I tell them.

"To the monsters?" Odysa says incredulously.

"That's what they do to keep them at bay," I say.

"Shh, there, there," Freya says kindly.

I give her side-eye. "I'm not your lost child, Freya." This just makes her lips curl further.

So, this is it then. Not the most climactic way of going out, but this is life, not a folktale. I cough, blood splattering out. "I think you know I have a secret stash. Food, weapons, medicines. Items that can help you pick a lock, somewhat fend off an attacker, and be replenished in isolation for at least a few days. I will tell you where it is, but only if you do one thing for me."

"What is it?" Odysa asks.

I suppress a groan, but a whimper comes out instead. I slap myself internally. "Flee this place with Colette," I state, my voice hoarse and wavering. They seem a bit confused and exchange glances as if to ask the other for an explanation that neither one has. "You must vow to it," I say firmly.

"I vow," Odysa declares.

"There's a loose brick in the wall in the privy, on the right side, adjacent to where the holes are." I narrow my eyes at them both. "If there is an afterlife, I know I am barred from ever entering; thus, my lost soul shall have nothing better to do than curse you with living misery until the end of your days if this vow is not upheld."

"Why should I entrust any of our well-being with words from the likes of you?" Odysa presses. She wants me to know that she knows I was the one who foiled their revolt, and even if I did not give her away this time with the window, my past actions are not pardoned.

"Odysa," Freya scolds her but she does not back down.

The pain becomes sharper and it's harder to speak. I muster my quickly draining strength and strain out, "Colette is my sister. She never knew her father because he was mine, old Igor the blacksmith. He confessed to my mother and my mother to me as he died of fever. And I may have no grace but she has all the grace in the world." I start quivering, the tremble taking over my entire body.

They seem surprised at my ability to be so sappy. Even I'm surprised. It's rather humiliating, to be honest.

Oh well. Soon there will be no more reason to preserve my dignity and reputation.

It's funny. Even now as I'm lying on my deathbed, I can't help but consider prioritizing such idle matters like how others perceive me. I chuckle a bit at myself. It comes out as a mix between a dry rumble and a hiccup.

Freya and Odysa exchange bewildered glances. I stop chuckling as the lump in my throat becomes more blatantly present and the burning becomes hotter in my eyes than in any of the large, bleeding gaps in my body. I swallow. "Tell little Etta..." I strain out, words impossible and worsened by how heavy every little reflex becomes.

"Yes?" Freya gently encourages.

I try again. "Tell Colette that, er... t-tell her that..."

$$\overline{\hspace{8cm}}$$

Chapter Three: Odysa

$$\overline{\hspace{8cm}}$$

All I can do is gape at Rowena. The way the blood streams out of so many sources on her body. It drips off of her and surrounds her corpse as if to frame her remains with color.

I'm getting used to staring at dead and bleeding bodies.

Freya is weeping. She scoots closer to me and rubs her head against mine, resting her neck on my shoulder, the closest thing we can get to hugging each other with how we are tied.

I don't know how to feel about Rowena. Sure, she helped me survive this instance, but I just know she had something to do with Yvette's revolt failing. There was just something about her wily smile and eyes that were so observant they were practically omniscient, paired with her obvious lack of care for anyone other than herself.

If I was as kind of a person as Freya is, I'd decide she was a living soul and did not deserve so brutal an end even if she sentenced so many of the people that I care about to something just as cruel.

But I'm not. And I can't tell if I think she is to be pitied or got what she deserved.

All I can do is stare at her, until finally I tear my eyes away, and let her exist just in my corner view.

According to her, the monsters are real. Could it be true? Can anything she said be credible?

We have no choice but to assume so.

I move my head away from Freya so she can see my face. Seeing as our hands are tied tightly behind us, we can't exactly communicate with the sign language Freya made up long ago, so she'll have to solely look at my lips. "I'm so sorry I got you involved in all this," I tell her.

She shakes her head. "It's alright. I-I just hope we can make it out of this. We *need* to get out of this. We must find Colette and somehow flee."

"We need to find Edgar and Liliana as well."

She doesn't respond right away, processing my lips and making sure she read them correctly. She tilts her head to the side and exhales. "Not this again."

"Is it truly far-fetched to think they're still alive and merely hidden away? You truly believe that the monsters came in one night and slaughtered everyone except for us? Why would they stop there?"

"Commander Ingrith's people might have been able to contain them and force them out again."

"They have the capability to force a retreat but never attempted any type of offense? Freya, they want us to feel isolated and alone. They want us to lean on them as our saviors, for then we will never question them and 'endanger' our safety. They need to be our only hope and sanctuary, and they cannot have that if we are holding out for something greater."

A new hope seems to take over Freya, a fire filling up in a body that has been swallowed in darkness for years.

I haven't seen that level of a raging fire in her since she first began to lose her hearing when she was five years old and the town doctor told her she might not have the same life as her friends. After she wiped her tears off, she studied and practiced with a conviction not even the most patriotic of soldiers have until she was beyond proficient at speaking and reading lips. Her parents often told her how proud they were of her, but no one was prouder of her than I was—her friend who was born 'lame,' grew up beside her, and always knew she had it in her.

"How will we have enough time to break out of this cellar, find Colette, find them, and then escape altogether?" she brings up.

I smile. She's asking the right questions now.

I look around, then spot my crutches on the other side. They're across from Rowena. Freya follows my eyes.

She's closer to that side, but she'll have to stretch past Rowena to get to them.

Testing out the length of the rope around her legs, she tries standing in place. But that's as far as she can go—even just a fraction of a step forward just yanks her right back. She sits down again.

Taking a long inhale, she swings her upper body forward so she is laying face-down and head-first across the room. Her head is right next to Rowena's, her shoulder already pressed into the sticky substance of her blood.

Her face is mostly obscured from here but I can feel the strain in her entire body to avoid Rowena. The crutches are just a little bit of a way above Freya's head. She reaches for them with her mouth, then her chin, but she is unable to get any closer.

She turns back at me.

"Why'd you have to be so short?" I quip.

In spite of everything, she can't help but chuckle.

She jerks her head at the broken bar next to my lame leg.

Perfect.

I rotate my back to grab hold of it with my hands and I do my best to toss it towards her with the limited movement.

It lands right on top of Rowena's chest. We both freeze, struck by horror.

Freya's forehead wrinkles up. She braces herself, and then turns her head and twists her body to face Rowena. Their faces are so close to one another that if Rowena were still alive, they would be exchanging breaths.

She gazes right into her dead eyes. A stifled, choked gasp bursts out of her and she pants sporadically.

"It's alright," I tell her, even though I know she can't hear or see me from here.

Still on the verge of erupting into wheezing sobs, she rotates her upper body and stretches it over Rowena's soaked, stiff body, where the blood has still not finished pouring out. She opens her mouth and hovers it right above her wounds, and then closes it around the bar, doing her best not to touch any part of Rowena but nonetheless getting her chin soaked in her blood.

Her lower lip is trembling so much that the bar jostles in her mouth.

"Careful," I whisper, more to myself than her, already predicting the worst.

Sure enough, the bar tumbles out of her mouth, rolls off of Rowena, and lands next to her opposite arm.

Freya just halts in place. A noise between a cry, a scoff, and a gasp comes out of her like she cannot believe this is actually happening. She now has no choice but to lay and rub up her upper body right against Rowena's body in order to be able to reach and grab the bar that is now painted with Rowena's blood. I can feel her crumbling inside, but she does it.

Then, she turns her head and torso in the direction opposite of Rowena, back to where the crutches are. She adjusts the bar, now gripping the end to give it a longer reach, and uses it to poke at the handles of my crutches and drag them towards her. She manages to bring one of them close enough to lay her chin on top of, and then pull it closer so she can grab it with her hands and slide it towards me. She repeats it for the other one, and now I have both my crutches between the two of us.

Eyes and nose glazed pink, her almost-entire upper body doused with the goopy red of Rowena's insides, she beams at me.

"Beautiful," I smile at her.

She shifts and rotates about until she is back to her original seated position. "Now what?"

***

"Dame Anice, please!" I cry out.

"What?" Anice says sharply from the other side of the door.

"I think you may have tied Freya too tightly. She can't feel her hands anymore. Please!"

I hear a heavy sigh and the clunking of a key being fitted through a lock. I nod at Freya, and she twists her face into a knot.

Anice comes in and closes the door behind her. "Let me see," she says as she squats down in the middle of Freya and me, her back to me as she examines the rope around Freya's wrists. I grip the long rod of one of my crutches, which I slipped behind my back. With Anice looking nowhere near me, I twist my torso away from her and swing right back into her, the rigid end of it crashing right into her spine.

She groans, wobbling as she rotates to face me. I knock my forehead as hard as I can into hers, feeling the reverberation in both of our skulls, and then swing my crutch into her one more time, this time against the back of her shoulder so that she crashes down in front of the two of us.

I waste no time taking hold of Anice's sword. I run the rope around my hands back and forth against the blade until it falls off; then, I grab the sword and slice the ropes off my legs and off of Freya.

Freya hands me my other crutch and I use them both to bring myself up. As she picks up the cut ropes and gags and ties her up, I crack the door open and peek my head out.

There's that one guard posted right outside the room that's just a short distance away from me. Another at the front of hallway.

I pat her pockets, plucking the key out and locking the cellar from inside.

"Window," I tell Freya.

We head over there and proceed to wiggle and tug at the bars with all our might. Anice's head lolls about and she groggily watches us, muttering something through the gag.

"Sorry," Freya mumbles to her, genuinely apologetic.

But I ignore her as I slam the hilt of the sword against the bar, making it hum and shake. It comes off, and the next, and the next.

Alas, enough bars are off that we should be able to squeeze through. The window easily slides open.

Freya goes first, sitting on the sill and swinging her legs out. She looks back at Rowena's body one last time, before she scoots to the side to give me room. I hand her the sword, my hands full enough with my crutches, and sit on the window. I bring my good leg out and grab hold of my functionless one and heave that over as well, the soles of my feet dangling four very high stories above weed-ridden grass and overturned stone pavement. I remember to slide the window back down and send Anice a final scowl.

I figured at this time, Colette would likely be in the library, so we move in that direction, westward. Freya stands up with her back against the wall and shuffles sideways. I don't think hopping side to side would be wise, so I stay sitting and slide along the ledges.

I forgot how crisp and alive the outside world was. How the wind likes to tickle your skin, how the sun likes to jab into your eyes and beam into your face, how the chill of the atmosphere likes to sink into your bones. How the scents of earth join together to create one distinct smell.

There's a low row of windows right up ahead. We sneak a peek into the first one. The room has a bunch of beds and tables, way more than needed, as I only count about six people—five of them with aging hair. I find myself fixated on them. I haven't seen anyone with greying hair or wrinkles since before Queen Hildegard issued the executive order.

Freya lightly taps my thigh with her foot, snapping me back to the present, and we continue shuffling, peeking inside before hurrying past each window.

Alas, we make it to one more, small window. Freya peeks her head in and then nods back at me in confirmation.

Through the bars, I see Colette wandering around the aisles, a slump in her step that I know only comes around in her most distressed moments. "Come on, get closer," I egg her on quietly.

She stays in the middle aisle, sidestepping out of view to look at the books there.

"Really, Colette? As if you haven't read all of those a dozen times already?" I mutter.

One of the other women goes to the third shelf, the one closest to us. Freya and I yank our heads out of view. We wait a couple moments, Freya glancing inside before she nods and I join her in the peeping, this last shelf clear of people again.

Colette pops into view again as she sets a book down heavily and—starts towards the door! No!

I tap my knuckle against the window.

It doesn't stop her.

I tap it one more time, louder.

One of the women—the same woman from earlier—looks up and around but upon hearing nothing else returns to her book. This catches Colette's eye and she wanders to the back of the room, towards us!

She runs her fingers over the tattered spines of the books, halting right before the window. Freya and I poke our heads into the very edges of the window, just enough for her to see us.

Her eyes widen. "Oh, my goodness," she mutters, leaning against the window. "I couldn't find you anywhere. I had no idea what to think." Her voice is faint from the other side of the glass.

"We're escaping," I tell her. I can imagine the shock that rushes through her, but it only manifests in the form of flickered eyebrows.

"You must go to the privy," I continue. "On the right side, there's a loose brick with hidden supplies. Collect them and come back here. You must break these bars and let us in."

"Let you in? Why don't I sneak on out?"

"It's far too high to jump from. And we need to find Freya's family."

She curls her lip doubtfully. I give her an insistent look. She sighs. "I'll be back."

***

I try not to lose my mind waiting for Colette. Freya keeps peeking back in, her foot anxiously tapping the ledge.

Then, I hear a faint voice, one that I do not recognize. It must belong to the guard. I catch "over" and "lunch."

Colette strides into view, the guard marching after her. "I do beg your pardon. I just need to find my mouse." I'm almost certain that's what Colette says, but I don't read lips as expertly as Freya and putting her already soft voice behind a pane of glass makes it impossible to hear her.

"You must leave now, peasant," the guard scolds, her hand going on her sword as she gets closer to Colette's back. My heart skips a beat.

Just then, Colette yanks a book off the second shelf and whips it at the guard. As the guard deflects it, she hops onto her back in a blur, wringing her arms around her head and neck in a chokehold. The guard takes a couple of wobbly steps before her knees buckle and she collapses to the floor, knocked out.

Freya looks shocked, but I just smirk. That's my Etta.

70

She had told me before that she grew up in the poor side of town, and there were periods in her life when she and her mother lived in the streets. She built a strong community with other street urchins, but there were frequent harassers, drunkards, thieves, and other ruffians that picked on them and would particularly take one look at her and decide she was an easy target. Hence, she learned to defend herself very well.

She closes the door and comes back to drag the guard behind the center bookshelf, completely out of sight, and then pops up again in front of the window. She pulls out a discolored sack from under her dress. It appears to be composed of a bunch of different cloths and rags sown together to make a large and misshapen quilt that Colette now clutches at the top to keep it all together, leaving a hole just wide enough to stick her arm through.

Tucking her hair behind her ears, she pulls out a set of plyers from the sack and bends down to fasten them around the corner of the window, straining and pulling. With one final grunt, there's a dull plopping noise, and she holds a rusty nail out. She repeats the process three more times, for each corner, standing on the sill to reach the top two, until each nail is removed and the entire set of bars comes out with a final heave. Her pocket bulges a bit, the mouse poking his head out before slipping back in.

She unhooks the latch and slides the window up, letting the two of us slip on in. I barely get my gatherings in place before I just about hop into her, and give her a good plop on the lips.

As she rubs my arm, she catches sight of Freya and her eyes nearly pop right out of their sockets. Freya's face flushes nearly as red as the bloodstains on her dress.

I hold her hand. "Later, Etta."

She shakes herself out of it and digs into the sack, pulling out another one of the standardized dresses they have us wear and handing it to Freya, who sighs with relief.

As she changes into it, I look at the guard's unconscious body, and an idea crosses my mind.

The dress fits Freya just about right, only dragging to the floor a little bit. But when she places the armor over it, stuffing the ends of the dress into the leg holes, the get-up works just as it should.

"Where to?" Colette asks.

I tie Anice's sword to my waist, covering it with my dress. "The north wing."

Freya dressed as a guard now, she grips Colette's arm and my shoulder and escorts us out. I feel the way her fingers dance in rapid trembles.

The traffic in the castle flows in the opposite direction as us, to the meal room. The guards stationed along their specific posts glance at us, but other than that pay us no mind. It seems Ingrith has not found out about our escape yet.

We make it to the other side of the castle, emptier and quieter. Freya nods at the guards, and they nod back, letting us go without another thought.

We cross into a large and vacant hallway at last. But then a figure invades the emptiness from the other side.

Ingrith.

My breath catches in my chest and we all turn in the opposite direction and go down another passageway, only to be met by two other guards right around the corner.

They look us up and down, their eyes sharp. My perspiration presses my handprints around my crutches, making the handles dewy.

"I'm escorting these two to Commander Ingrith," Freya says.

"Oh, alright," one says. They have no reason not to believe this, especially considering how nonchalantly the guard that approached me last night after dinner and walked me to the cellar was, and how nonchalant Freya is now.

But the other guard does not waver.

"What's your name, again?" she asks Freya.

"Freya."

The guard examines her and then us.

And then they reach for their swords.

I yank out the sword from under my dress, letting one of my crutches clatter to the floor and balancing on my good leg as I block one of their blows. Freya pulls out her sword and parries the other guard barely in time.

The guard charges at my leg. I stop it with my sword and rotate the sword to twist her arm downward, and then I ram right into her face with my shoulder, sending her chin flying up. I punch the back of her head for good measure, sending her crumpling to the floor.

Freya's hands are empty—two swords in that guard's possession—and I almost scream as the guard nearly runs her through—before Colette trips the guard, sending her down on one knee. Before the guard can orient herself again, Colette takes out a thick and long nail and slashes it across her face.

"They're here!" that guard yells at the top of her lungs.

Colette and Freya start running. I bend down to collect my crutches and start towards the swords, but the guard drops her hand over her eyes to swing at me with the two swords, and I hop backwards. "Odysa, come on!" Colette urges.

"Say no more!" I exclaim, abandoning the swords and moving the hell out of here with them. I can already hear a flurry of footsteps and clanging armor heading our way at full speed. I throw my head back, and there's already six guards after us. A minute or so later, and there is a dozen of them.

"Turn here!" I direct us, making a sharp turn into the next passageway, where the staircases leading up and going down are.

"Yvette said there are servants' passages on every corner of the first floor of castle," Colette says in between pants. "If we head that way now, we can probably make it to one!"

She starts running towards the stairs going down, and I start after her before I realize Freya has stayed rooted in place, looking at the floors going up. "Go," she tells me, waving her hand.

"Freya, no," I say.

Colette looks down the stairs impatiently, a subtle bounce in her steps. "There's no time."

"We'll come back for them," I assure Freya. She looks lost and torn, as if the stitches that are keeping her together are unspooling on two opposite ends. I take her hand and give it a strong yank before I use my crutches again. Colette glances at our interlocked hands—very quickly and subtly but I catch it.

Freya and Colette run down the stairs, turning back at me. I sit on the railing and slide down, making it down before them.

The clanky chorus of rustling armor bellows behind us, the stampede of a dozen guards led by Ingrith. "Stop!" Ingrith shouts.

Halfway down my slide down the next set of stairs, something sharp thuds into my leg—my good leg—sending me catapulting off the rail and tumbling down the stairs, my crutches clattering down after me.

"Odysa!" Colette exclaims.

I look at the arrow poking out of me, throwing my head back at Anice, whose bow is still drawn back. She inserts another arrow in, Ingrith and the others running in front of her, at the head of the stairs now.

I start to push myself up, but the arrow makes every bit of pressure on my leg spark up the entire limb. Colette and Freya each take hold of one of my arms and legs and carry me hurriedly down the rest of the way.

Another arrow whizzes just over our heads. "There!" I call out, pointing to the servant's passage.

It's more like a tunnel than anything else, since it's so dark and dingy and just one straight and narrow hallway. There are no lights here, except a small sliver of daylight at the end, the beacon of hope we need it to be.

They set me down as we reach it. I rattle the knob, which is of course locked. Colette heaves her body against the door. The guards are closer and closer; I can hear them, and I can see the outlines of their silhouettes invading us more and more.

The door pops off the frame, off-kilter, light and the outside world blinding us as it floods inside. We are now standing in the border between the castle and the open courtyard, the path to a whole other world from a lifetime ago. We can see the abandoned buildings of the ghost town that once was our bustling kingdom.

I start outside, when an arrow lands on the frame of the door right next to me. "Stop in the name of the Queen!" Ingrith yells shrilly. She has her sword up, her army behind her, and is just the length of another sword away from us. One quick charge and she can impale us like bonfire meat on a spit.

"There is no queen, Commander Ingrith. It's just you. And pardon me, but we fear you not," I say.

"You will die out there," she states.

"Better than in here," I reply. I spit on the floor while glaring at her, and get the hell out of here.

I wince with every forced grounding of my leg against the broken pavement of the courtyard to keep the rest of my body going, my knuckles turning white with how hard I grip my crutches, trailing behind Freya and Colette only slightly as I force myself to go even faster, and they stop and wait every couple of steps.

Something tells me we can somewhat afford it now. I throw my head back; Ingrith is standing behind the broken doorframe, just watching us run.

There's a faint ringing in my ears, so distant it could be dismissed as the wind. Colette looks at me, and I know she hears it, too. We go to the first building we see, only to find it is boarded up.

The ringing gets louder and louder, and I look around frantically but I do not see anything other than phantom streets and rundown houses with broken windows and boards or even ones that are just a couple months away from caving in.

The ringing is like a quiet shrieking in my ear now, not much louder but more present and poignant than before. Visceral and almost tactile. So close I can almost feel the source of the sound itself.

Colette snatches my arm and leg, Freya quickly following. "In there!" I exclaim, seeing a well-standing and open house across the street. They run, my body jostling in their arms. The ringing gets louder and louder, and now there are steps accompanying them, but still no sign of them any direction I glance. Rapid, running, galloping steps that are getting louder and louder.

They rush me inside and slam the door shut. A second later, there's a slam against it, and the wood pulses backwards. I push my body against it, fighting to compress the pounding and the pulses that give the door a heartbeat, a tormenting life that haunts us. Colette dumps out the contents of the sack and runs against the door as well, pulling out a hammer and rapidly hitting nails into the frame.

The drumming moves to the walls of the house and there are scratches at the doors and windows, which have already been boarded up so that the glass is completely obscured by wooden panes nailed against it.

There are silhouettes on the ground under the doorframes. The hair rises on my arms. Freya glances at our gawks at the door and soon she is gawking as well.

The pounding and scratching stops, but the high-pitched ringing continues on and the shadows on the ground do not leave.

They've never felt so close before—or so real.

"They're out there, but I don't believe they're trying to get in anymore," I say. "We should be somewhat safe."

Whoever lived here must have wanted to keep their home safe from any of the lingerers who stayed back despite the executive order to loot the empty and unguarded buildings. There had been a lot of word about such occurrences the first couple of nights those five years ago, and some must have been smart enough to think ahead.

Well, it's a shame for this owner, for the door had been busted wide open, the shelves and drawers were left opened, and they seemed to have gotten effectively ransacked. Nothing remains except the bare bones of the house—the chairs and a table. There are a couple other rooms besides the living room, but they are both empty. There is an old bed remaining in one, but it is merely the wooden bed frame.

I limp over to the kitchen table, resting my leg on a chair. My leg is stained with streaks of blood.

There are only two chairs here, and I take up both of them. Perhaps I should be more courteous, but all things considered, I think I'm entitled just this once. Freya kneels in front of my leg.

Colette picks up some bottles and cloths from the floor that fell out of the sack and sets them on the table. Freya squints at the different bottles, sliding the one she used on me yesterday closer to the edge where she is for closer reach. Colette stands behind me and puts a hand on my shoulder.

In the midst of the pile of little knick-knacks from the sack, there is a thin book. *A Condensed History of Orienne*, the title reads. Colette brought it with her. A final remnant of Yvette.

The thought of Yvette seems to conjure up something inside of me, like a quiet humming turning into the earth-shattering buzzing of a bee swarm. I try to swat them away, but now they are all stinging me at once. Each sting has a name and a face attached: Yvette. Amabel. Ravinn. Lella. Rosa. Rowena…

I notice Freya is looking at me. She is asking for permission. I brace myself and nod. She grabs the arrow and yanks it out. "Curse you!" I screech, Colette hugging me from behind. Back in the castle, I had to hold back, but now not even the blur of a consideration passes through me.

Freya may not be able to hear but she knows exactly what kind of words are spilling out of my mouth right now. Even so, she knows it's nothing personal. She pours a bit of the medicine directly onto the wound, making it singe.

She dabs at it with the cloth. "You're fortunate," she says. "It's not deep and not serious." She unties the ribbon around her wrist.

"What are you doing?" I ask her.

She presses a new cloth against my wound and winds the ribbon over it and around my leg until it is tightly fastened. "You should only need it for a day or so."

"If it were any longer, you'd let me bleed to death?"

She laughs, but it is hollowed out by a graveness. One that has nothing to do with me but with everything else.

"It will be alright," I tell her. "Once we get our heads on right, we'll figure out how to get your family. They're not expecting us to survive, and they'll certainly never expect us to return."

The edge of her lip twitches up, but the rest is held down and made immobile by the thoughts holding it hostage. "I best change out of this get-up," she says, gesturing at the armor. She pats my hand and heads into the room with the bed frame, closing the door but leaving a bit of a gap.

"So," Colette says, moving in front of me, "we made it. Can you believe it?"

"Not in the slightest."

All the events of today run through my mind, and it all feels impossible. This all has to be a vivid dream. Part of me wants it to be, but the other is praying I don't dare wake up if it is.

But here comes yet another nightmarish part.

"Colette, I have something I must tell you," I say. "Rowena is your sister." Bafflement and surprise flicker through her eyes. "Or half-sister."

"I—pardon?"

I hold her hand, patting it with the other one. "Let me start from the beginning. Ingrith had Rowena locked in the cellar with me. She tried to pin Freya as having inside information in the revolt."

"Sounds like something she'd do," she whispers, still ensnared by shock and confusion.

"But then Freya and I tried to escape by breaking the bars off the windows. Ingrith caught us, and Rowena backed us up. And Ingrith killed her." Colette's eyes dart side to side across mine, and I watch the moisture build up in them.

"As she was dying," I continue, "she told us where her secret stash was and told us to flee the castle with you. That's when she confessed of her relation to you. She said your father is hers, old Igor. The blacksmith."

Her forehead wrinkles up, her face reddening. A couple harsh and jagged weeps tumble out of her before she grips her mouth, squeezes her eyes shut, and forces a large inhale and exhale. The release of her breath is jagged and pierced with the cries that threaten to overtake her but she fights it. I hug her, rubbing her back.

Colette takes a couple moments to compose herself, keeping her breathing steady. "You can cry," I tell her. "I'll be here."

She shakes her head, like I thought she would.

"I never asked my mother about my father," she says. "She had enough to deal with, so I didn't dare burden her. From what I pieced together I knew I was born out of a thoughtless affair." She rubs her eyes, drying her tears. "I often passed old Igor's smithy on my way to the marketplace, but I never had a reason to go in there. I never met him. I hardly even know what he looks like. But it's not as if I ever needed anything from him."

"I'm sorry, Etta."

She sighs. "Even if we are family, why would I matter to her? Why should I be any different than the stranger next to me?"

"Well, I suppose it may be as simple as that," I suggest. "There are very few things left to care about in this world, that when you find even a hint of one thing, you sure as hell better protect it with your life. Perhaps that's what she was doing." I shrug. "But who knows? It's impossible to sort through anything that went on in her mind."

She wipes her nose off and nods. She hardens ever so slightly. "Is there anything else you need to tell me?"

I know precisely what she is referring to and I reply without hesitating. "Freya and I grew up beside one another. We were the best of friends in our childhood. When we became older, we spent a week together romantically. But it was not to be; our personalities were too opposite of one another for it to last. Hence, we went our separate paths. She found her love—and I found mine. I care a lot for her but *you* own every inch of my heart."

"Alright," she says.

"Really? I pour my soul to you, and that's your response?"

She leans in, pausing halfway through to peer at my eyes. I close the gap between us, making each meeting between our lips slow and lasting, hoping she feels every fractal of love I am sending her way. For I feel everything she is offering me.

****

Around suppertime, we open up the sack and look at the food in there. A couple slices of bread, two carrots, and four fruits. Colette picks up a pear, staring at it closely, and then bites into it.

This definitely isn't meant to last for an extended period of time. Not between three people. We could very easily go through this right now and still be hungry. But if we try, we can probably stretch it to at least two days.

I take the apple, chomping down on it, hoping it will do something for the hollowness in my belly.

We eat in silence, like we have been the past couple of hours.

The mouse runs out, and Colette drops him a couple crumbs. As he chews, Colette rubs his head with her finger. Then, he scurries away again.

"Seems like a bit of an unfair arrangement," I say. Colette looks at me questioningly. "He comes in to get food from you, just to be on his merry way again."

"Are you saying *he* should bring *me* food sometime?"

"He should give you some form of compensation. Freya, you agree with me, don't you?"

She grins. "It seems only fair."

83

I raise my hand up, in a 'See?' gesture. "At this point, he owes you quite a big debt. If he doesn't start paying now, I don't know what will become of him."

Colette's brows scrunch together. "Alright, Odysa," she plays along.

The three of us exchange glances and then just burst out laughing at the ridiculousness of it all. Freya bows her head down, covering her mouth. Colette's is silent but her body jerks up and down and her eyes twinkle. I just throw my head back and let it all spill out of me.

We start to calm down, then look at one another and it begins all over again. Eventually, we let out any last remnants and sigh in contentment, the smiles lingering over our lips as our bodies relax.

Then, a sudden burst of sadness strikes me like a tidal wave into a fisherman's rowboat. It's as if *everything* has popped out from nowhere and I'm now drowning in it all.

I wish we weren't stuck in a random house all on our own, surrounded by some sort of monster or evil force or who knows what.

I wish my friends were here. I wish they were well. I wish I didn't watch them fail and die.

Colette reaches over and squeezes my hand, offering me a small smile. I cannot say whether or not she noticed the strange torment inside me, but either way it comforts me. The cloud is still there and I am still entangled in it like a fly in a spider's web, but I remember it is not the only thing here. The rest of the world does not cease spinning over one storm cloud, no matter how dark and tumultuous it is.

Being alive, being human, is hard and messy but with all the twists it can't help but throw you something good every so often.

I send Colette a smile back.

"Well, it's rather early, but I am beyond slumped," I say. "I'm uncertain about you two, but I elect for sleeping on the floor. That bed frame looks like it actually *can* cut me." Freya smiles, and I just realize I inadvertently left Colette out of an inside joke. She smiles, not seeming to mind, and I hope she truly doesn't.

"I call the quilt!" I exclaim as I grab the corners of it, letting all the objects lightly roll off, and then wrap it around myself as I lie down.

Freya laughs and rolls her eyes.

"So much for chivalry," Colette remarks.

"If you wanted it, you should have been quicker."

She pushes my shoulder, and I push her arm back.

"Fine, I suppose we can share," I say, exaggerating each word.

She chuckles, lying down next to me, nestling her head into my shoulder. I look up at Freya, snuggled in the corner, eyes closed. I glance at Colette and she nods in agreement, so I toss a chip of wood at Freya. She opens her eyes. "Want in?" I offer.

She smiles and shakes her head.

"Freya," I scold endearingly, "you will enjoy this washcloth blanket with us."

She chuckles, examining us timidly before coming over and sneaking in next to me. It covers about half of her body and half of Colette's. The areas of scraggly material rub up uncomfortably against my skin, making it itch. It almost makes me miss the sheets back in the castle.

I rest my arm around Colette, leaning my head against hers, soaking in her warmth, the rising and falling of her chest hypnotizing me into sleep.

When I wake up, I close my eyes again, trying to prolong the sleep as long as possible before the clanky bell forces us up. And then I remember.

Odysa's arm is heavy over me. I burrow my head further into her shoulder.

She's strangely stiff, stonelike even.

No.

My heart jumps into my mouth.

I don't want to open my eyes. I squeeze them tighter shut.

But the longer I stay here, the colder and harder she feels and the deeper the grave chill that has appeared out of nowhere inside me crawls into my body. I flutter my cyclids up.

She's pallid and hollow and vacant.

She's as transparent as a phantom.

It's like someone has poked a hole in me, for it's as if I can feel the life draining out of me. I stare at her, dumbfounded.

My jaw drops, but I am so numb I do not even feel it. Next thing I know, I'm on my feet, but I might as well have levitated here. I am as far away from myself as she is from me.

Freya has now risen and is gasping at Odysa, same as me, shaking her head frantically. "No, no, no," she blubbers as she puts her fingers against Odysa's neck and then her wrists over and over again. She takes off the sorry excuse for a blanket and lifts her dress up, exposing her leg with the wound. Her veins pop out, black as charcoal, a greenish tint outlining them, surrounding the cloth.

Freya's fingers quiver, making each motion take twice as long, as she unties the ribbon and removes the cloth. Under it is the center of this haunted web, a dark and bright and ugly nest.

I bend down, suddenly unable to breathe, tears crashing out even as no sound escapes me. Freya turns back to me, mouth wide open and twitching.

"You—!" I strangle out, the tears suffocating me. "You—said—it—wasn't—deep—or—serious!"

"I didn't realize the arrow was poisoned." Tears stream down her eyes. "That must be the poison Rowena stole from them. That's why they were so incensed with her. It's no ordinary toxin." The shaking in her voice gets faster and rougher and her cries stick her words together like goo, making it an effort to understand her. "It's insidious and stealthy."

"You said it was nothing to worry about!" I whisper sharply. My knees buckle and my eyes start to droop. I grip the wall, shaking my head wildly, fighting it as sobs from the pit of my soul throttle my entire body in rapid bursts. "You said she was going to be fine! You-you—"

My eyes roll back and I drop the rest of the way down. I vaguely feel Freya throwing her arms out, breaking my fall, before sleep conquers me.

***

When I wake up this time around, there is no moment of confusion. Not even a fraction of a moment where I am stuck in the margins of reality. It hits me all at once the second my eyelids groggily flutter up in a giant and merciless attack, like a predator just waiting to pounce.

I sit up, breathing deeply, but my throat is tight and my chest is all wound up.

Freya is sitting next to me, knees tucked in tightly.

The quilt is strewn over Odysa's body, covering her head and going down to her calves.

I bring it down and examine her face. Her rich brown skin with white patches, moon-kissed speckles on a polished canvas. Her soft coils of black hair like swirls of clouds. Her plump lips that offered me sanctuary and refuge time and time again. Her soft jawline that I would rest my hand against to kiss her and to hold her.

Freya holds my shoulder. I have been dancing on the edge, and this little gesture almost makes me fall over the edge and break down again. But I quickly regain composure. I squeeze her hand, covering Odysa's face once again.

It's so strange.

I am sitting next to Freya in an abandoned house in Orienne with my lover's body on the other side. Yesterday, my half-sister died in a cellar, and the day before the woman who had become something of an older sister to me—along with everyone else I had eaten with nearly every day for years—lost a revolt.

It's strange how life brought us all together.

I'm fairly certain Yvette was a noblewoman, someone with good-standing wealth and prestige behind her name. She never let it on, but I could tell from her intellect and manners. A person can have either naturally, but the air of her movements had such a specific level of dignity that at least part of it had to have been ingrained in her and raised with her.

Before all this, I only saw Odysa and Freya a couple times in the city. I would often pick up words about them that got sprinkled through town—the "deaf one" and the "gimp." It always made me wonder what words were being spread about me, if there were any.

I caught sight of Rowena a few times in the streets, her reputation preceding her. She was in the stockades more than once after getting caught stealing. There were a couple times she passed through the poorer side of town, and we would lock eyes very briefly before she tore hers away and walked faster.

I got to know these people I never would have known before and take a poke at their souls, and they at mine. Who would have thought we would become as entangled with one another as we did?

And now I've lost them all.

Months of meticulous planning just for Yvette's revolt to fail instantaneously. Turbulent fighting and forceful running amidst the blood and sweat that soiled our bodies and minds just for Odysa to die as soon as we make it to safety. Years and years of distance from the family I never knew just for the only one left to leave the moment she takes a step closer. A small flame of hope lit in the darkness with the howling winds doing everything they can to blow it out, but we all do our part in nurturing it, covering it with our bodies so our spines receive the cold beatings instead, until it finally grows into a light strong enough to power the world... just to be knocked over at the last minute.

I'm sorry. I project the thought into the void, hoping each one of them catches it.

"Tell me something about her," I say suddenly. I realize Freya has not processed my words at all, her mind nowhere near her head. I tap her shoulder, bringing her back down. "What's your favorite memory of her?"

Freya thinks for a moment and wipes her eyes. "One that comes to mind is when we were rather young." She sniffles. "I don't remember what we were doing—I might have been coming up with new words or we might have been playing—but a few young boys went up to us and proceeded to tease us. They mocked us; one in particular made a grand show of waving his hands exaggeratedly and pretending to limp, the rest of them laughing as if he was a royal jester. I was on the verge of tears."

Her lips peel into a smile. "And then Odysa went right up to him and punched him in his face." A bright huff of air escapes my nostrils. "She broke his nose. I remember telling her off like a mother scolding a child. But she merely dusted her hands off. She assured me we would not get in any sort of trouble since they would be too ashamed to let anyone know that they had ran away fearfully from the 'cripple' and the 'deaf girl.'"

"Was she right?"

Freya nods, grinning.

"That sounds like her."

"Tell me yours," she says.

"Mine would probably be the day we met," I say, thinking back to it. "We were first acquainted with one another in that dining room, a year or so after the executive order was issued. It was also the first day I came across that mouse." I point at the hole in the wall. "He had somehow crawled into the room, and I noticed he was grabbing the crumbs from under her table. Odysa saw the mouse and was about to smack him with her crutch, so I stepped in and told her not to hurt him. And then the rest was history." Freya smiles.

'Is it yours?' Odysa had asked me then.

'No,' I had responded.

She waited for me to elaborate to no avail. Clearly annoyed and with Yvette and Amabel sitting across her and watching all this unfold with much amusement, Odysa barked, 'Alright then, well, can you just keep it away from me?'

'I just told you, he is not mine. I cannot stop him from doing whatever he wants,' I answered calmly.

Odysa was close to boiling over at this point. 'Then why can't you let me get rid of it?'

'Why are you itching to kill him? You were the one leaving a feast for him,' I had said. We examined each other up and down, and the only thought in my mind was how beautiful this ill-mannered oaf was. Something softened between the two of us.

'Now, now,' Yvette had told us off, a secret twinkle in her eyes as she looked at us.

Odysa glanced at the crumbs on the floor and said, 'I *was* making a bit of a mess, wasn't I?' A smile broke through both of our faces. Odysa had chuckled and Yvette invited me to sit with them.

That was *the* moment for me. The moment that defined everything else that followed. The moment that brightened that dim, windowless room and the decaying palace of Orienne.

Suddenly, I realize I've been thinking about this in all the wrong ways.

Yes, damn this cold, cruel world. Yes, it deserves to shrivel up for taking her too soon, for taking all of them too soon.

But it's not about how they died; it's about how they lived. It's not about what they did or didn't do; it's about who they were. It's not about how the world treated them; it's about how they lit up the world simply by existing.

To only look at their sufferings and shortcomings and decide their lives summed up to nothing but tragedy would be a great disservice to everything they were as people. I knew their smiles, felt their joys, danced in their fulfillments, and soaked in their achievements. Their lives were overflowing at the brims with goodness and wonderment, even if it wasn't in the ways they may have been seeking.

"You know, as we got older, we drifted apart," Freya goes on bittersweetly. "Soon, it reached a point where we would just greet one another kindly from a distance. There was no particular reason; it just happened. So, I'm truly thankful we had the chance to be friends again before…" She sighs and dabs at the corners of her eyes. "She always seemed to be doing well, though, and then I was courted by my husband and had my daughter, so I was certainly

93

happy as well." She smiles wistfully, but not like she is mourning the memory—more so like she is reigniting it.

She is clutching this false hope dangerously tightly.

"I'm sorry," I say, "but I don't think the chances of them being alive or you making it back to them even if they are, are very high." Her face falls. "And if you're recaptured, you are dead for certain. You don't want to waste the life that's been given to you." It's more fragile than we think.

"I won't pretend your words have no credit," she says. "But I don't know if I can live forever with this gnawing uncertainty."

"Well, you must consider if the slimmest sliver of a chance of living a life that includes your daughter and husband is worth the nearly *certain* possibility of death, the end of everything."

"I don't know. But wouldn't you risk it all for...?" she trails off.

A tense and awkward silence builds up between us.

I get up and sort through the remaining food. There's just two pieces of bread and an apple left. I saw the apple in half with a shard of glass (the sharpest item we have on hand) and distribute the food between us, sitting back down. A couple moments later, the mouse runs out from inside the wall and climbs comfortably onto my lap. I sprinkle a couple strips of bread down to him, and he picks them up with his little claws and eats.

"We can't stay here," I say.

"You're saying we ought to venture out? Where the monsters roam?"

With everything that's happened since I woke up, I didn't even notice that the ringing has been absent all day. There are no shadows under the doorframe either.

"Do you think it's just you and me out here?" I say, not really talking to her or to anyone, more so just throwing the question into the air to see where it lands.

"You think there might be others hiding out somewhere?"

I look at the ransacked home we are in, think about the other buildings that have been boarded up. "Not everyone obeyed the executive order. Some must have stayed behind. Perhaps they're still alive."

"So," she says, her eyebrows raising in slight passive-aggressiveness, "you find it more likely that people who have been out here for five years among the monsters have survived than my family?"

"I think the human spirit is much more resilient but also much frailer than we think."

Her brows furrow, not quite following my argument. "You're saying my family is frail?"

"No. Just that a life can endure so much but still be snatched away in an instant. Life aims to surprise the one who holds it." The mouse gets off of my lap, carrying the last piece of bread, and retreats into the hole in the wall. "I know you wish to find your family, Freya, but we have to weigh the risks and the likelihood of each outcome. I would never suggest going outside if we had any other choice besides stay here and slowly rot away."

"How do we know they won't simply ambush us the moment we remove the nails from the door?"

"Because I don't hear anything." Freya looks even more uncomfortable, and I realize this might have sounded more like a jab than I meant it to be. She is so good at reading lips that I often forget she can't hear.

"We need to leave soon, while it's still silent," I say.

"Shall we just leave Odysa here then?"

I scoff. "That's just her body. She's already long gone."

She shrinks.

"Are you with me?" I ask sternly. "I am pushing to get out of here because logically it's our best shot, but truly I have no idea what awaits us. If we are doing this, I need you to be with me all the way."

Her eyes jump to the mysterious door, Odysa's covered body, the scraggly lace around her wrist, and then land and stay on me. She nods.

***

I pile all of the little objects from the stash onto the table. There are two more nails left; some wooden, faceless figurines; a few silver and golden coins; a set of plyers; a hammer; a couple spoons and forks; five spools of thread; some pieces of cloth; a small ball of yarn; sowing needles; different bottles of medicines; a few hairpins; a spade; and two makeshift blades constructed out of a large, abstract piece of glass tied around a wooden shaft.

Rather interesting and arbitrary items Rowena collected over the years, but these are her life savings.

How did she even come across all of these?

I can imagine her snatching some of these from people's pockets, but some of these are impossible to just randomly happen upon. She would have had to know about them and seek them out herself.

I suppose she really is just that good at finding her way around.

And then of course, there's the book, which I've decided not to bring. It's the practical thing to do, as it will only take up extra space and weight that should be reserved for useful things. But it's not just that. In a way, it would feel almost unfair to bring along the last remnant I have of Yvette and not of Odysa. If I can leave Odysa's body behind, I can leave a set of pages behind, too. I don't know why I even had the impulse to bring it in the first place.

Were you feeling sentimental?

Freya has been sitting beside Odysa's body and holding her hand over the quilt, keeping her as covered as possible. I walk up to Odysa's body, Freya's hand going back to her side, and I know it is so she can let me have my moment.

But I don't take the chance she is giving me. Instead, I briskly roll the quilt off of Odysa's body and bring it back to the table. Freya's eyes cast their own shadows upon me even as she tries not to.

I flatten it against the table, stack all the objects onto it, and fold the corners inwards to transform it back into a sack, twisting and fastening the top of it. Freya stands up and goes into the bedroom, closing the door behind her.

I sigh. What would she have me do, hold everything in my arms so they can all topple off one by one as we run around the unknown?

Odysa haunts me in the corner of my eyes, but I refuse to look at her. I don't need to trace over this empty corpse; all it will do is chill my soul, which I am already fighting so hard to keep alive. I don't need to scour her remains to squeeze out one final reminder of her, for I already know what she looks like. I already know what she feels like. Her touch is forever ingrained into my bones, the echoes of her fiery voice—fiery in the way it simultaneously warms those she cherishes while stinging those who threaten them—forever ringing proudly in my ears as my national anthem.

I bend down and peek into the small hole in the wall, setting a small piece of fruit by it. If I listen closely, I can hear some scurrying in the distance, but the sound does not come closer.

I always knew he was a free animal and we were going to part ways at some point. "Goodbye," I whisper. I hope he survives long.

Freya comes out of the room. She lingers beside Odysa for a couple more moments before joining me. I hand Freya one of the blades and a thick nail. I grip tightly onto the other blade, the last nail in my pocket.

Using the pliers, I wiggle and pull out each nail from the doorframe. I press my ear against the wood, listening closely. Nothing but rustling winds.

I turn to Freya, who is quivering. "Ready?"

She gulps and nods.

I open the door, and it creaks softly on its hinges. Outside, it is just the empty and abandoned town. I step out, Freya following closely behind and shutting the door behind her.

Leading the way, I head down the street towards a building that appears to be boarded up. There's a sign hanging above the door that has rusted away, but I vaguely remember it. I believe it used to be a bakery. I never had enough money to eat from here, but I can almost remember the fresh aroma that used to trickle out.

I grip the doorknob, and it is as stiff and held in place as a dead body. I pick up a stone from the ground and bash it against the window, the glass easily shattering, the stone making the wood twitch before it bounces back to the ground.

I poke my head in and scan inside.

It's just a bunch of chairs and tables. It appears the bakers must have brought everything of worth with them, and any leftover ingredients are long gone by now—not even the ghosts of their memories remain.

I slither my head back out, careful not to scrape it against any glass, and lead Freya further down the street. I look around and see a house that also looks firmly locked up, wood covering its windows.

As we work on tearing the wood off, I start to hear a faint ringing. My stomach twists.

I tap Freya's shoulder. "I'm starting to hear them," I whisper.

Her eyes widen, her face blanching.

I move faster, just about rattling the wooden board I'm holding. The ringing plays in my head like soft background music, as if we're inside a pub and there's a couple of live performers. Except this song is tone-deaf and ominous and makes my skin crawl. I look around, but I see nothing but our lifeless kingdom.

We manage to rip one board off—thank goodness—leaving a sliver that is just big enough for me to slip into. "Keep working," I tell Freya, and I slither in through the gap before she can protest.

Cobwebs greet me in the dark gloominess of the house. I brush them off with one hand as I open the sack and rummage for something that could be of use. What we need is an axe. The closest I get is the hammer and the plyers. I use both to try to tear the nails off, but they are sunken into the wood. There is no hope in pulling them out; I must break the wood itself. I look around at the furniture that is encrusted with dust and spiderwebs, and the fireplace behind it. An idea flashes in my mind.

I take out the wooden figurines from inside the sack and rub them together quickly. A tiny flame erupts from the friction. I bring it over the wooden board, blowing lightly on it so that it grows. I cover my mouth and nose from the fumes as it eats the wood, crackling and sparking. I slam the melting and splinting wood with the hammer, making it easily fall down in a pile of flames on the floor.

On the other side of fire and smoke, Freya is gaping at this sight. I grab the tablecloth off the table and throw it over the fire, stomping on it roughly until it becomes a sped-up march and the fire dies out, but not before consuming the majority of the cloth along with the wood.

Freya's ghostlike face relaxes as she sighs with relief. I wave my hand in, and she joins me inside, taking a look at the mess on the floor and raising her eyebrows.

I gesture at the table and we lift it together, turning it on its side so it leans against and covers the broken window, keeping us at least temporarily enclosed in here, and hopefully the monsters temporarily enclosed out there. "Let's just grab what we need and go," I say, wiping the sweat off my brow.

We stick together as we open drawers and explore rooms. All the decorations and paintings of this home are intact and in good condition, even if dust is slated over them like newly fallen snow. The paintings are of flowers and open meadows, and there are a couple small busts and figurines of Queen Hildegard and the Queen before her. My eyes only pass over everything briefly as I am well aware of the time crunch, but I can't help but notice the small cracks on one of the busts, the way Queen Hildegard's hair is chipped off the top as if her hairdresser slipped and cut off too much.

There's a vase on a stand in the corner, a standing clock that is forever stuck at eleven-fifty next to it. There is an oval-shaped frame hanging in the middle of the wall, the portrait taken out so it is nothing but an abstract void now. There are three beds, each one in its own room, and I wonder what kind of family lived here.

Seeing nothing but dishes and decorations in the kitchen, Freya and I go inside the biggest room, which I assume belonged to the parents of the household. I open the wardrobe, and while half of it is vacant, the other half still has clothes hanging from it. I take a couple capes, one a tranquil blue, the other a neutral brown, both of which are embroidered with lilies. I quickly fold them up neatly and set them inside the sack.

In front of the boarded-up window is a desk with ink and quills placed neatly in the corner. Next to the desk is a bookshelf with cobwebs blanketing the shelves.

I sift through the books, tracing my fingers over the texture of their leather covers, the dust glazing my fingers. I pull one out with a particularly wrinkled spine and flip through it. In the middle of it is a map of Orienne; a couple pages later is a broader map, each distant area of land on the map labeled something different. Then, about two-thirds down the page is 'Orienne.'

"What's that?" Freya asks, leaning in and examining it closely. "Are these… other kingdoms?"

It's honestly quite terrifying how little we know of the world outside our own, how indifferent we had all been to this lack of knowledge for so long, always being too comfortable with what we knew—until that became uncomfortable as well.

"Freya, do you think the monsters migrated from those other kingdoms?"

She tilts her head. "Possibly."

I look further down the map, at the bottom of the page. It seems to be an area of unclaimed land, past a series of mountains, out in the open and rolling meadows by the ocean. While it still seems rather distant, in comparison to all the other kingdoms, it is much closer.

A thought occurs to me. If I were to operate under the assumption that this map is actually accurate and not just a series of imagined illustrations, then this place could be a haven, a sanctuary for people like us. The mountains would serve as a natural barrier of protection, with the other side being safety and paradise. Farther down the ocean coast seems to be another kingdom—so that even if this new area failed, we could try assimilating into that other kingdom.

I take the bottle of ink from the desk, wincing as I force the cap off and dip one of the quills in it. I draw a circle around that area on the map. "Could this be where everyone has gone?" I wonder aloud, Freya watching my lips. "Perhaps they followed another map there?"

"Who knows?" she says.

"Odysa always thought there were others out there. Maybe she was right all along."

I write 'Odysa' next to the area I circled. I read a lot better than I write, but that is the one word I can do in my sleep. It was the first thing I asked Yvette to teach me how to write, before even my own name.

Freya watches me closely, deep in thought.

But before either of us can think on it any longer, the ringing has gotten louder. Much louder—like it is coming from the other room. I hear clawing and rummaging just outside the hallway.

I tear out the page and stuff it into the sack. I peek out into the hallway just in time to see the table collapse upside down, and shadowy figures appear at the windowsill. My heart jumps to my mouth.

I shut the door and snatch Freya's wrist and yank her close. "Hide," I whisper to her. The color drains from her face and she jerks her head about frantically before she rushes inside the wardrobe and shuts it behind her. I drop to the floor and crawl under the bed.

I hear movement just a little bit outside the door, the shredding of wood as something sharp drags against it by multiple sources at the same time, and of course the ringing that is excessively loud and close.

The clawing and shuffling noises are right against the door now, and I resist the urge to give into the shaking and crying I am so closely teetering towards. Then, the door pops open, swinging unevenly on its hinge with a loud creak that is like the cry I can't release.

And then I see them.

They are positioned in exactly the perfect angle that I can see them for exactly what they are.

They are massive—they would hover over horses—with bodies of gigantic lizards, and coated with scales like armor. Their bodies are as long and thick as the trunks of trees, their four legs just stouter trunks that extend off of it. They have five claws on each foot painted as black as ravens' wings that are like daggers, both in length and threat; they slice into the wood just by standing in place. They have tails that are nearly as long as the rest of their bodies that coil and swish like snakes, like they have their own consciouses, autonomous from the rest of the body. A line of bright spikes, like rocks at the bottom of a cliff, run down to the end of the tail from the top of the head.

The head... it is the culmination of every horror these monsters entail. Pointy spikes flare off the ends of it like a mane. The muzzle is long, round, and dense. Their fangs, only slightly shorter than their claws, hang out of their enormous jaws like stalactites and stalagmites. The tip of the bottom of their jaws drags down, finishing the jaggedness of their faces and bodies. Their nostrils are like a set of black pits to fall into, never to be seen again. Their eyes are the same color as the rest of their bodies—they are either a dull grey or green through and through; there's barely any color in them and they easily blend into the background of the rest of the world—so the eyes merge into the rest of their figures except for when they blink or when the small pupil darts about.

There are about five of them in here, and the one who leads them has a gigantic spike protruding up on the end of its muzzle.

The ringing trickles out of all of them. As they go inside the room and get closer, their bodies are obscured and all I can see are their thick legs and their unbelievable claws.

They surround the bed, and one of them stands right before my face. I grip the blade even tighter, my own nails digging into my palm.

One leg swings under the bed, and I slide backwards before the claws gash my face. The monster retreats its leg, and then its horned face appears before me.

I stab the glass right into its small dark pupil, making it wobble backwards and screech an ear-piercing screech. I hobble out of the bed, Freya bursting out of the closet, and we duck and dodge past the screeching monsters and their swinging legs.

Its comrade is right on our heels, and I snatch the vase off the stand and whip it right at its face, disorienting it for a brief moment. Freya knocks the standing clock over, making the rest of them hesitate for another very brief moment, just enough for both of us to leap over the window and bolt.

We run with an unparalleled intensity, bolting into another open, rickety building and shoving the door shut. The door shakes, the monsters pounding right against it, cracks splitting through the wood. It will give in any moment now.

Abandoning the front door, we burst out of this house through a side door and continue running through the streets.

The ringing elevates into screeches, and the slapping of dozens of feet against upturned pavement and dirt is so loud it's like the monsters are right on top of my ear. But I can only catch glimpses of them as they duck into the shadows and between buildings; the flashes I do catch of them are so brief and blurry they could easily be hallucinations.

My breathing is deteriorating into rough and sporadic wheezes. How could it not be? This was my plan, and everything I feared is happening, and now we're about to—

No. I need to calm down.

We just need to find a place where we can hide. I just need to focus on that.

We run through the town square, and I can't help but peek into the open smithy where old Igor worked away, a foul smell wafting out of there. But when Freya looks in, she gasps and skids to a stop. I almost scold her when I follow her gaze. I see the moving outlines of more than a couple beasts in there. And then I'm met by an unimaginable sight that turns my arteries to ice and cuts my legs from under me.

There are piles of bodies in there, human bodies.

Some of the bodies are decomposed or close to it. One pile, the one close to the entrance, has not yet decomposed. The bodies are mutilated and sliced open every which way, but there is a certain closeness to life in their dead faces, as if they can still open their eyes and stand up and dance.

My breathing picks up again, my heartbeat slowly veering out of control, tears striking my eyes, and I can already feel my body weakening.

No, no, no.

I shake myself off, pulling Freya, but she is rooted in place. She is shaking, gaping as sobs burst out of her.

Fury suddenly overtakes everything else in me. Here I am, doing everything I can to contain myself and Freya is not even trying.

I hold her face. "You need to get it together," I tell her. "I cannot have you drag me down. Or vice versa." I do not know Freya well, but if I were to lose consciousness, I just do not see her leaving me. No, she would likely just pick me up and carry me until she got eaten. And I cannot have that happen to her.

Freya nods, biting her tongue and abruptly halting her cries. I grab her hand and continue running.

The screeches are louder than ever, and the next glimpse I catch of the monsters is between the buildings right next to us.

All of a sudden, the horned one dashes out from behind the buildings in front of us, blocking our path, the wooden handle of the blade still sticking out of its eye. We turn in every side and direction and angle, and now *eight* others have emerged out of the darkness to surround us in a perfect circle in the middle of the street. A circle that only gets smaller and smaller as they get closer and closer.

Their forked tongues slip out of their mouths. Their nostrils flare. Their claws drag through the pavement, tearing through the stone with every step.

The only thing that is included in this quickly shrinking circle is the main town well, shadowed by a wooden roof with rickety pillars that a long rope hangs off of. Freya and I exchange glances.

She holds up the glass on her dagger so that it intersects with the rays of the sun and flicks it into the eyes of each of the monsters.

As their screeches turn into aggravated cries, Freya and I bolt towards the well. There is no more water in there; it's just a long and empty hole with a bucket at the bottom, tied to the end of the rope.

The horned one has recovered already and rushes towards us. I throw the nail I have on hand at it as if it's a dart; it bounces against its fang, chipping it slightly and making the beast cry out.

Freya and I grab hold of the rope, and I slam my feet against the rickety pillars of the roof, Freya following suit. Just as the other monsters start approaching, the roof collapses downward, covering the well and rushing Freya and me into its dark depths.

Far up above, the creatures are shrieking and clawing at the wooden roof. Freya and I climb down, our vision adjusting to the pitch-black just in time for our feet to hit the dirt.

"What now?" Freya asks, her voice wavering.

I don't know. My only plan at the moment was to get away from the monsters, and this was all that was offered me. I pat around, feeling the cemented stones, not quite sure what I'm looking for. A secret pathway? A hidden stash?

A slice of light enters, the monsters having succeeded in shifting the roof to the side. Freya frantically touches the stone and the ground, tears running down her eyes as if they're racing against one another. The slice of light grows, shining enough for us to see everything with stark and blazing clarity.

I stop patting around, and a couple moments later Freya does, too. She puts both of her hands over her mouth, gripping the bottom half of her face, doing her best to contain herself.

I take a deep breath.

Alright, I think, understanding the situation.

"Alright," I murmur under my breath, accepting the situation.

I put my arms around Freya, and she squeezes me tightly, her entire body jolting as she weeps into me. I move my hand behind her head, lightly and soothingly stroking her hair.

I'm terrified, regretful, and so damn disappointed I cannot begin to describe it. But I also have enough of my bearings together to know that there's nothing else to be done. There's no use fighting it. And at least I don't have to be alone in this.

My heart aches with a grief that cannot be deciphered, but it is as calm and steady and gentle as the waters of a lily pond. Shrieks of defeat echo in the open forest of my soul, but a most peculiar tranquility quiets it down like a mother shushing her wailing child.

A million thoughts scramble through my mind, but I blow them away as if they are nothing more than crumbs on my polished plate. I don't want to think of anything except the way my body is condensed against Freya's, compressing us into one unbreakable unit.

It doesn't matter who we were or weren't to each other before now. Because now, we are all we have and we are all we know—just like it had been with Yvette and Odysa and everyone else. As they all enter my thoughts—even Rowena—the serenity and peace that had been budding absorb everything else inside me. I may not have lived the perfect life that I had idealized, but how could I be unhappy when I had found everything I needed, all when it mattered most?

I smile, sighing contentedly.

My darling Odysa, I am glad to not have to spend much longer missing you.

Freya and I sit down and kneel, still embracing each other tightly, as full daylight conquers us and I hear the distant thud of the roof off to the side, the scraping of claws against stone, and the now-deafening screeches. The space rapidly condenses into claustrophobia; she hugs me tighter and I hug her tighter as well. I feel five large slashes against my back at once, and we fall over, now laying against the ground. I roll my body and hold Freya tighter, the monsters tearing through us but neither of us letting go of each other.

I adjust my eyepatch carefully so it is snug against my face. My eye and the area surrounding it no longer sting, but any whoosh of air, even just one generated by people walking by, still irritates it. Hence, the eyepatch.

It's a stupid way to lose an eye. Stupid but effective. There's the sharpness of the nail, and the dirt and rust collected around it so that if the slicing doesn't do the job, the contamination will.

I tie my hair into a tight low bun. That villager put in a lot of effort to escape just to storm right towards death anyway. It's been long enough that I don't necessarily wish her ill will, but I still don't wish her anything good. But I will say if she was going to run right into the monsters' lair, she could have done that without taking my eye as another casualty.

I check out my reflection one more time. The large window at the top of the guards' accessory room lets a large amount of light in and is not hindered by any bars or curtains, maintaining a constant high state of illuminance. It is bright enough to pinpoint every flaw and beauty mark on my sandy skin, but if I rotate my body at a specific angle, the rays of light can also sear through the imperfections and turn them into blurs.

My chestnut hair is right in place, except for a few stray hairs that slip out rebelliously no matter what I do, as if to taunt me. I run my palm over them, flattening them down, trying to make them fade into the rest of my sleek bun or at least appear to.

Satisfied, I set down the brush and walk past the rows of guards, each doing final touches in front of a mirror. Then, I realize I spent far too much time here, and unlike everyone else, I am about to be late.

"Good morning," I say politely to the guard that is standing in front of the accessory room. I greet each of the other guards I hurry past, exchanging courteous nods, until I make it to the meeting room with time to spare.

Commander Ingrith is sitting on the chair in the middle of the room, while everyone who is currently not on duty stands around her. I spot the top of Lavender's cherry-blonde hair and place myself next to her. She smiles, and then her eyes move towards the top of my head before she points at it. Sighing in frustration, I just take the whole bun off and start all over, tying every single hair in place this time.

A couple minutes go by, Commander Ingrith tapping her fingers on the arm of the chair. Then, she speaks up. "I'm certain many of you are aware that it is time once more; I only mention this because I have had a couple of you approach me, asking if we were still carrying on with business as usual. Now, I understand that this is the longest we have gone without hearing the monsters' screeches, but the last thing we should do is assume we are safe and the monsters are no longer hungry. We gave them quite a feast those four weeks ago, which is a good thing, for as you all must have noticed, we are reaching a shortage of the elderly and sickly population. We will soon have to start picking people out from the general population, and I have begun compiling a list of people for then. Tonight, we shall clear out the sick ward."

I know we never meant to last long here, that our doom was always slowly impending, but suddenly it feels closer than ever.

"Dame Isolda, come hither," Commander Ingrith says. "All else are dismissed. Carry on as usual."

I head on over, everyone else streaming in the other direction out of here. Commander Ingrith's eyes stay on my eyepatch for an extended moment, and even though it's been about a month, it still makes me cringe.

She reads off of her list. "Marsily," she says. "Bring her to the sick ward so that she may be taken care of."

"Marsily the madwoman?" I clarify.

She nods.

I'm honestly surprised she hasn't been done away with already.

She's fortunate to have lived under our administration.

"Anyone else?"

"Perhaps we can start reducing the number of people we sent out," she says. "If so, this should be fine for tonight."

I curtsy and then exit the room.

It doesn't take long for me to find Marsily.

She has rich skin, a wide nose, and average stature, and she is sitting on the floor crying as she cradles her knees and rocks back and forth. A woman with dark brown skin is rubbing her back.

I stand back, waiting until the situation stabilizes, knowing I am in no position to intercede in the midst of all this. After a couple minutes, she stops rocking, rubs her eyes, and sits normally. The other woman leans in as if to ensure she is alright, and then the two of them just lean against each other and talk.

I give it a couple more minutes before approaching.

"Marsily?"

She looks up. "Yes, madam?"

"You must come with me."

"Why?" she asks, nose scrunching in puzzlement.

"Just come."

"What shall you do with her?" the other woman joins.

Why must they make this so difficult? "She is exhibiting symptoms of a sickness that is spreading."

"Sickness? What sickness?" Marsily asks frantically.

"Not much is known about it yet; it is very novel. We only speak of it in scattered whispers so as not to create panic and disorder." I tilt my head down, conveying seriousness. "If I hear any word of this going around, there will be repercussions."

"Pardon?" Marsily says, shaking her head. "I assure you, I'm no different now than I've always been. I've actually been doing quite better recently, if you're referring to my fits of madness."

"I am not. Come now."

"What symptoms *are* you speaking of then?" the other woman asks. For crying out loud. "If you don't mind me asking, madam. I spend so much time with her; I could probably verify your information if needed."

"You are not privy to such information."

"But—"

I hold Marsily's arm, gently yet firmly calling her to her feet. Her eyes widen and her eyebrows arch, a cry for help. "Madam, I promise I feel fine," she says desperately.

"When will she be back?" the other woman asks.

I tug Marsily away.

"Please, madam," she says, following me.

I lean in towards her and drop my voice to a clenched growl. "You are on the verge of losing your next couple of lunches. Our judgment is not on trial. If the rest of the castle gets infected, it will be on you. Now back away before I make you."

"It's okay," Marsily says to her.

She looks at her, worry and defeat transforming her face. She is caught at a loss of what to do, like an animal in a snare, and I can see her already standing on an unending path of self-hatred as she backs away slowly and lets us go.

I start to bring Marsily away. She looks down at the floor, her forehead like a wrinkled piece of parchment. "I'm going to die, aren't I?"

"It will be alright," I say flatly, the same way I have every other time.

"Can I have a minute with her?" she asks.

I think for a moment. "Yes," I decide, "but please don't dawdle."

When I let go of her, she walks up to the woman, and they hug each other tightly.

"You're the best friend I've ever had," the woman tells her softly.

This whole scene has caught the attention of a couple bystanders. "Keep moving," I snap at them.

I wait patiently for them to finish up. Alas, Marsily comes back to me and lets me take her away. I lead her to the end of their section of the west wing towards the area only permitted to us guards. I move her past the cellar and into the sick ward.

She takes a good, wide-eyed sweep at the six women inside, particularly the elderly women. "Where are the medicines for me?"

"The only medicine you can receive now is rest. Savor the rest of the day."

"*The rest of the day?* That's all I have left?" There's a snappy edge in her panicked question, making the words less 'that's all I have left?' and more 'that's all you're giving me?', like she knows. Knows that the sickness that is sentencing her to death is not hers, but that of the world she lives in.

"It will be alright."

Marsily looks right into my eyes in a way no one else ever has, one that is so daring and so knowing. Her hooded eyes just blaze right through me, as if my body is no longer made of bone and muscle but transparent glass that reveals everything inside and behind. Fear and sorrow swirl through them, but they are merely clouds against the dark night that is raining a lightning storm of disgrace, disgust, and shame upon me, soaking and crackling me.

"Don't look at me like that."

"Like what?" she says, not stopping. She knows the odds are stacked so high against her she is but an ant in comparison, but she is still going to make this as dragging and difficult for me as possible. Even if she can't do anything to stop or slow any of this, she knows she can play with my mind and my conscience, for I am but a mere mortal trying to do what I know is the right thing. What all of us guards have the duty to do, things that no one else has the courage or strength for.

"Life is cruel for a person like you. Where you're headed is going to be much kinder for you, and you'll be a hero for all those here," I reason with her.

"You're absolutely right, madam," she says, but her stare only intensifies. "After all, you guards know best." Her eyes get watery, but they only magnify everything happening inside them. "Anything to fulfill Queen Hildegard's word. Anything for Orienne."

I strike her across the cheek, making her cry out. Then, I march out of there.

Goodness, did she irk me! What nerve!

I march all the way to the storage room, the guard standing before it sliding to the side to let me in, clearly reading the frustration on my face and not wanting to delay me any further. I head in, thousands of barrels and boxes taking up the large space (thankfully, we are impressively organized). I walk past the clothing, extra tools, and miscellaneous sections towards the extra food section in the very back. It was put there to discourage going into it, but like everything else that is here, it only makes sense that we get the opportunity to access them when needed. After all, our jobs are incredibly stressful and can take quite a toll if we are not careful; the least we deserve are a couple little things to take our mind off it all.

And this way, all the villagers have at least partially paid their debt to us by having their past belongings now be put to better use by us. It's the least they can do for us, and it's not as if they are in need of them.

I take out a pouch of sunflower seeds and chew on them. The door creaks open, and Lavender enters. "Oh, hello there, Isolda!" She notices the tension in my face. "Rough day?"

"They can be so irritating sometimes."

She nods sympathetically. "Here. Last week, I found a couple fun items in here." She goes into the miscellaneous section and pulls out a plushy ball that is about half the size of her hand. "What do you think?" She gives it a couple squeezes.

I take the ball, squeezing it over and over again. A couple moments pass, and I'm no longer as heated as before.

"Strangely meditative, isn't it?"

"It is."

"Eve would probably play with it."

"You think so?"

She shrugs and nods.

I glance at the ball and tuck it into my pocket. It bulges ever so slightly, putting it at risk of falling out. I shove it down further, and it seems a bit more stable now.

I sit on top of one of the barrels. She hoists herself up next to me, and we eat out of the pouch together.

"You know, you're right. Sunflower seeds truly are an acquired taste, but once you acquire it, it's just the right amount of crunch and flavor," she says.

"Told you."

She chuckles. "Aren't you due to stand guard soon?"

"Damn, you're right!" I hand her the bag and hop off.

She snorts. "I truly admire your punctuality."

"I always manage to arrive on time."

"Yes, because you have to run to get there."

I laugh, hitting her arm. "Don't start."

"You're about to be late; you don't have time to start anything," she quips.

I point a finger at her. "We'll continue this later."

We both chuckle as I leave the room and hurry to my stationed corridor in as dignified a speed-walk as possible.

***

As night falls upon us, all the women are led towards the makeshift dining room for their dinner. Meanwhile, a select number of guards—such as myself—walk past this room, past all the hustle and bustle of normal life, to the ward.

There are a total of seven women in here. There's Marsily the madwoman and one other lady around her age who has been in here for quite some time, always seeming to have a cough or fever. The rest are elderly women who are reaching their time on this earth anyway.

They are all that is left of what this room used to be.

Commander Ingrith stands at the head of the room, handing us rope as we head towards each person.

A small old lady with short hair grips tightly to another woman, stepping away into the corner of the room, their backs against the barred windows—ah, yes, the twins.

The others do not move, seeming to have just accepted this. After all, they saw the people around them slowly get led out. With no one else left, they know it is now their turn.

Falling in line with everyone else, Marsily stays still as I tie her wrists and ankles up and set the gag over her mouth. But her eyes follow my every movement closely, their intensity only interrupted by blinks. I look back into her sad eyes that continue to try to shame me, suppressing a sigh.

"Who are they, Maud?" the woman in the corner asks her short-haired twin, her voice trembling as Lavender and another guard approach them.

Maud pushes her sister behind her as Lavender gets close. "Let her go!" she shrieks at the guard reaching for her sister, whose eyes are bulging now as her head swivels side to side at everything happening around her. Maud squirms and strikes Lavender square in the face.

At this point, Commander Ingrith has shown up beside all of them. She flicks her head to the side, sending Lavender away and she steps towards these sisters, her shadow sending their faces into darkness. She snatches Maud's wrists and binds them roughly so the rope cuts into them and shoves the cloth into her mouth, making Maud gag.

Now that everyone is tied up, we usher them into a single-file line; they stumble and shuffle awkwardly in their restraints. We allow the elderly woman with a cane to keep it—it would be cruel to not—and she balances her cane in the middle of her body, resting her hands on them. One of the women is in a wheelchair, and we simply wheel her forward, her tied hands resting on her lap.

Tears run down all of their eyes. The women with a cane and a wheelchair glance at each other, sending secret messages with their minds. The other young woman keeps her eyes pasted on the floor. The long-haired twin seems to have already forgotten her fear, for she simply glances about and hums into the gag around her mouth. The other three women—the twin, Marsily, and an elderly woman with wavy hair and unforgiving eyes—glare sharply at us guards.

"It will be over before you know it," I tell them quietly. "Just think about the life you were able to lead before this, and how many lives you will allow to continue because of this."

Their glares do not soothe out, and now it is time to lead them down the hall towards the grand entrance, that familiar ringing sounding loudly in my ears.

But we are still inside the sick ward. We are not yet anywhere near the grand entrance. This ringing is too close. Far too close.

Suddenly, the door to the ward bursts open. A couple guards come spilling in, panting harshly, horror on their faces. Commander Ingrith opens her mouth, clearly to scold them, but they beat her to it. "They're here!" they cry in unison. "They're inside the castle!"

Commander Ingrith's eyes widen, her jaw tightening. "Leave them for now," she orders, waving us out.

All us guards run out after her, a couple staying behind to lock and guard the door.

As we hurry towards the grand entrance, Lavender and I exchange glances. Her arched eyebrows lower questioningly. I widen my eyes in return, both of us at a complete loss of what to think.

Then, once we make it there at last, pure nightmare-fueling shock captures us all. My blood runs cold, my heart skips a beat, and my legs turn numb.

Hundreds upon hundreds of the monsters are here, inside the castle, herded right before us all in the grand entrance.

There's someone at the very front of all of them.

"Is that—?" I whisper to Lavender.

"It can't be."

But it is indeed a woman of short stature, black hair, and angular eyes that dart nervously but now with a sense of daring in them.

It is none other than the deaf woman that tried to escape.

"I do not come to bring harm, but to make peace," she calls loudly, her muddled voice echoing. "Let's have a civil discussion. No blood need be shed."

Commander Ingrith is the first to interrupt the silence that has fallen among us from the shock that has dug into our bones. "Aim your weapons!" she calls, and those with arrows lift them. The creature right beside the woman, a horned one, twitches forward but she places her hand against its neck and it stays in place.

"Fire!" Commander Ingrith yells, and arrows fly towards the monsters.

But they merely bounce off of them, clattering uselessly onto the floor. I feel like I might be sick.

"Not the beasts!" Commander Ingrith says.

With that, I rush towards Freya with my sword held high, the other guards a couple steps behind my bold charge. At only a couple feet from her I start to swoop my sword down upon her—but the horned beast jumps on me, bringing me down in a blur. Its claws dig through my armor; slice through my shoulders, collarbones, and chest in ten places; and impale me into the floor so that I am stuck to it. I gasp, tasting blood in my mouth.

"Isolda!" I hear Commander Ingrith's and Lavender's shout, and it sounds like the world has silenced.

But for the first time in a long time, I'm hardly paying attention to Commander Ingrith. I'm hardly paying attention to anything happening in the castle, or even to the ten waves of stinging and suffocating pain. For the monster's head hovers right above me, blocking the rest of the world; right now, its jagged face, its long and pointy fangs, its slithering forked tongue, its earthy and barren scales, its tiny black holes for eyes that eat into my soul—that is my world now. I am no longer in the castle, or even in Orienne. I am in this monster's hell.

"No!" Freya yells. It sounds like she's slapping her thigh, and the monster turns its head back. It bares its fangs once more at me, revealing an even deeper level of perdition with its hundreds of large teeth, before casually hopping off. The claws all slip out of me at once, evoking a sharp groan out of me.

I moan in pain, Lavender running to my side. But even if the monster's face is nowhere near me anymore, it is all I can see now. Even as Lavender holds my cheeks and turns me towards her, those devilish eyes and horrific fangs are all I can see.

Chapter Six: Freya

"Stop!" I form the word forcefully, feeling it bounce from the back of my teeth to my lips, shaking my head and striking the side of my right hand down on the palm of my left.

The horned creature stays in place, seeming to process this before nudging my hand with her head. I stroke her head, simultaneously bowing my head in shame, apology, and condolences to the fallen guard.

***

I had woken up with a start, sweating and moaning from a terrible nightmare. I had seen everything all over again, all the blood and horror and suffering from people I once knew and some I even knew well.

But I was in an even worse nightmare now.

I rubbed my eyes, everything excessively bright as the light reflected sharply off of every rusted stone inside the well. I was so exhausted and groggy and disconcerted; there was only one thought in my mind, one that took over everything else: *How am I still alive?*

Colette's body was slumped on top of me, covering most of my body, from her head that was resting against my shoulder to her legs that were bent over mine. Her arms hung loosely over my sides, the same way mine couldn't help but fall from their tight grip around her when I crossed over into unconsciousness.

Except she was…

No. I refused to even finish the thought.

I had to get out of here. My body felt sore and tight and there was a stinging over my shoulder blade.

But that meant I had to remove Colette.

I put my hands over her shoulders, increasing the pressure little by little, as if I was about to wake her from her peaceful slumber. "Pardon," I said, finally holding and lifting her ever so slightly, just enough to allow me to slip out from under her, the loss of warmth from the weight of her body making me feel cold and excessively light, like I could float away if a strong enough breeze came in.

My eyes were on the ground, on the imprints of my bottom and legs against the dirt I had scooted across until I was sitting with my back against the cold stone. The stone sent a chill and a sting through me when the flesh of my shoulder blade touched it. I turned my head as much as I could and saw the large slashes torn through it, like a rake through fertile dirt.

The rope was sprawled about in a messy pile, next to the turned-over and cracked bucket. It likely got cut by one of the monsters' claws or spikes as they hurried in. There went my only way out of here.

Then, I did the thing I was avoiding, the thing I least wanted to do.

I looked at Colette.

Her back was opened up. There was nothing inside but bones. She couldn't have even have passed as a ragdoll, for there was no stuffing inside. It was all gone. All eaten. Everything about this compassionate, strong-willed, fearless human being disregarded. How cruel was that—to not only have the audacity to sentence her with death, but give her one that treated her life so meaninglessly when it was everything but?

The first couple of tears escaped my eyes, and I just started sobbing.

Why hadn't I met the same fate?

Then, I remembered all the bodies we saw in the smithy, some of them looking hardly a couple days old. The monsters must have just eaten a feast. They weren't starved when they saw us. Colette had been more of a snack than anything else.

And then I realized I was alive because of her. She had turned her body in a way that shielded me and exposed herself to the monsters that came in.

I grabbed my hair and wept even harder. Damn it, damn it, damn it!

I cried so long and so hard my temples drummed and my eyes ached. The light coming in had faded into a duller shade. I would have kept on if the cuts on my shoulder blade didn't turn into a sharp and deep attack.

The sack of supplies was just a little away from Colette's hand, but now it was more just a poorly put-together cloth, laid out unevenly with a bunch of random objects scattered over and around it. Nearly all the medicine bottles were shattered, all their liquids having soaked into the cloth, the dirt, and the capes that Colette had grabbed for us. The light blue had stained into a dark twilight, the calm brown into the mouth of a dusky cave. The map was still crumpled up in a tight ball, the slivers of its corners torn and discolored, Colette's circle still standing brightly even if the edges were slightly smeared, along with Odysa's name. I touched the letters, sobbing even harder.

There was only one medicine bottle that hadn't shattered completely and still had some liquid left. It was next to my makeshift blade.

I stared at both, not sure which to grab.

Why am I still alive?

I didn't have the strength, courage, cunning, or fighting abilities that Odysa and Colette had. I didn't have a plan or a strategy, and even if I did there was no way I'd ever have enough of whatever I needed inside to execute it. I would rather die in here than go out. Even if I did go out, there was no way I would survive longer than a couple minutes.

If Colette and Odysa couldn't make it, how was I supposed to? They were the ones I depended on; I only ever followed their suggestions, never having anything substantial of my own to allow our survival.

I didn't even know that much about medicines, to be truthful. I only knew basic first-aid procedures since I practiced so much on Odysa when we were both young due to her experiencing her fair share of falls. I practiced even more when Liliana started running; she was such an active and playful child.

Oh, Lili…

I ran my fingers over the lace on my wrist. I had no idea how it was still there. By all logic, it should have fallen off or been reduced to nothing even close to its original state long ago.

My face heated up and more tears fell out of me.

What was the point of life? Do we merely suffer and struggle until one day it all ends?

Why hadn't I thought to rotate my body to shield Colette? I was a couple years older than her and a mother; I should have been the one looking out for her.

She was the one who was ready to conquer the world. She and Odysa would have ruled it.

And now I had the responsibility to make Colette's sacrifice worth it. Damn, I hated that. I hated it from the bottom of my soul. For I was not capable of that! I was the last person in all of Orienne who had the power to even partially make up for what Colette did for me. The world was not made for people like me.

I reached for the blade, wincing. But I grabbed the cracked medicine bottle instead. I didn't even have *that* in me.

After I poured the medicine down my shoulder and tore the bottom of my dress into strips that I then wrapped tightly around my wounds, I leaned back against the stone once more.

Then, I scooted towards Colette. I picked out a needle and thread from on top of the cloth and did my best to sow her together again. My fingers quivered as I did my best to ignore the lack of organs inside her body, the dried blood on her skin and dress, the careless and reckless manner in which she was torn up and broken. I laid the blue cape on the ground and gently rolled her on top of it, grabbing the ends and wrapping them over her. I pulled the hood over her petite face, covering her forever.

I rubbed the tears from my eyes, so tired of crying. So sick of the hole in my heart.

I stayed in there, just sitting and sleeping and tracing my hand along the dirt, for the next two days. Hunger and despair twisted my stomach even as I tried to ignore it. On the second day, the hunger got so strong it seemed like my stomach was bubbling. I just laid down and closed my eyes, opting for sleep instead.

I woke up to a giant whoosh of air coming from up above and shooting downward. I opened my eyes to see the horned beast inside the well with me, on the other side of Colette. I froze, my blood running cold, unable to move.

It was on its side and struggled to get to its feet, shaking itself off, the makeshift blade still poking out of its eye. It seemed to have accidentally fallen in here.

I squinted up into the dark sky, only partially lit up by the moon and the stars. There were three monster heads peeking their heads into the well, watching from up there. One of them hopped in, its claws keeping it steady against the stone as it started to climb down. The horned one looked up at it, and it stopped in place against the wall.

It faced me, baring its teeth and opening its mouth widely, probably making some sort of roar but obviously nothing I could hear. It shut its mouth, seeming to be confused at the lack of impact that had for me, and then started to go towards me before stumbling off-balance like a drunkard.

I glanced at the blade, still positioned nicely beside the medicine, just half an arm's reach away. The creature lifted its leg up threateningly, ready to claw my entire face off with one swipe, but then it wobbled and finally fell on its side.

I looked at the creature before me and all the others watching me from above. All of a sudden, they weren't as scary as they were before. All of a sudden, they weren't monsters. Just creatures trying to get by.

I slowly set my hand against her head and stroked it. She relaxed under my touch, succumbing to my comfort, and closed her other eye. I put my hand around the wooden handle and yanked the glass out in one quick and unhesitating motion.

She jerked harshly, her tail slapping the other side of the stone, her legs kicking out, her claws gashing through the stone. The creatures up above bared their teeth and hopped a bit, like they were preparing to ambush. My heart jumped to my mouth as I lifted my hands in a no-harm-intended gesture. The creature lifted her head up at her comrades and they all stopped in place. She laid her head back down again and closed her eyes.

I took the medicine and poured the rest of it over her face, her body only jerking softly now. I tore off another strip of my dress and tied it around the creature's eye, stroking her head and face. I felt a vibration that seemed to come from inside her mouth, like the strings of a lute when plucked.

A couple of her scales had torn off from when she fell in, revealing a layer of hide underneath that was also very thick and hard, but from which a black, gooey substance trickled out of. I softly dabbed at these cuts, her body caving in with a big sigh.

At the end, she rose to her feet, far towering over my miniscule figure and stared at me. She came closer and went behind me, her rough face against my back. I tensed up, subconsciously bracing for her to open up my wounds and scour for my insides. Instead, a bumpy and sand-like tongue ran over my wounds, soaking through the cloths I had tied and soothing the pain. Then, she climbed back out, the others following her out.

In the late afternoon the next day, she climbed back in. I scooted back against the wall, my body uncontrollably tight and constricted, hands shaking more and more the closer the creature came. She stood in front of me and opened her mouth, a big bean-shaped object dropping out and onto the ground before me.

It looked like a kidney.

She rolled it towards me until it was right before me. I cringed as she cocked her head at me, waiting expectantly. Was she offering this to me? What would happen if I didn't take it?

Gulping, I took hold of the kidney, her eyes following closely. It was coarse in my hand, close to withering away, its foul smell invading my nostrils and making vomit collect in my mouth. Not wanting to hold it any longer, I extended it to her, but she did not make any move towards me. I patted my lap, continuing to hold it out, and she leaned her long neck inward. Her tongue slithered out, wrapped around the kidney, and coiled it back into her mouth.

I wiped my hand against my dress, trying to eliminate that sensation from all sources of my memory. She stood in place and just stared at me; I couldn't tell if it was out of curiosity or if she was planning how to eat my own organs.

She turned around, the bottom tip of her tail rubbing against my jawline, my spine tingling. She stepped over Colette and dug her claws into the stone, starting to climb back up. She threw her head back and glanced at me, as if she was trying to figure out what I was doing, if I wished to climb on up as well.

I pointed up towards the sky and shrugged, my hands inadvertently landing on top of my thigh again, her head following them closely again. Then, she swiftly slid back down onto the ground and went down on all fours like an invitation, all the spikes along her spine contracting and disappearing.

I licked my lips. This could not be happening.

I could not sit on top of the creature that brutally murdered my friend and entrust it with my survival.

But what did I have to lose?

I glanced at Colette one more time, commemorating her and manifesting goodness for her, as I stepped around her and sat on the creature. Hoping I could manifest some semblance of goodness for myself as well. Hoping that I wasn't about to die from sheer stupidity. The creature leapt up along the wall, my body whipping forward, my hands flying around her rough neck as she climbed out of there.

She trotted through the town, slipping behind buildings and bouncing off of the walls between them, always under the cover of the shadows and moving in a stealthy blur.

The smell of filth and death wafted into my nose, and I saw once again the piles of bodies inside the smithy—where she was bringing me. I hopped off, rolling like a log for a couple moments from the height. She turned around, cocking her head at me, seeming to be confused.

She ambled up to me, leaning her head down close. I cautiously set my hand against her head and ran it up and down her scales.

Another one came out from the smithy. He looked at the horned one and then at me, opening his mouth. A small, grey-tinted sack fell out onto my feet. Not again. I picked up the organ and extended it towards him. Hesitating, he wrapped his tongue around it—just to drop it at my feet again. He came closer, watching expectantly. I couldn't help but tense up.

I carefully reached my hand out towards him, and he came forward to meet it. I felt the same vibration, albeit a bit slower, rumbling from his mouth as I stroked his head. Then, an idea popped into my mind.

I picked up the spleen, tracing it through the air so that both creatures were watching it, and pointed downward. They didn't seem to understand, so I pointed down again and sat myself. I pointed down one more time. The horned creature looked away from the spleen and examined me closely before deciding to sit down. The other one glanced at her and then joined us on the ground. I rolled the organ towards the center of them.

I just taught them a trick. I just taught the vicious monsters that capitulated our kingdom and ate thousands of people alive a trick.

The horned one stabbed the center with one of her claws and tore it in half between the two of them.

She stretched her body out, and I mounted her, strangely no longer as afraid. A couple of the other creatures came out, and it was hard to tell where they all came from, for they seemed to have appear out of nowhere. She turned away from the smithy and dashed through the town until we were outside it, where the woods lied. She brought me deeper into the maze of trees, circling around their trunks as well as bushes, as if presenting them to me. Some of the creatures had trailed behind us.

I caught sight of a hoard of berries growing on a string of bushes, and I couldn't help but jump ever so slightly from excitement. She slowed to a stop, and I stroked her head and hopped off, hurrying towards the berries and eating the whole bush, the torment in my stomach finally calming down. Beyond these bushes was an open meadow filled with tall grass and flowers, a sort of hidden paradise.

I spent the next couple days ambling about town on my own. I found what used to be a popular inn, its door swinging off its hinges and its insides filled with dust and cobwebs. But the beds were still there in their former glory, so I curled up in one and buried myself under the old sheets. When I wasn't sleeping, I filled my time with the company of these creatures; the horned one sought me out daily, others joining in occasionally. They seemed to seek comfort in the shadows and in the way they could disappear into the background if they wished; it seemed like they chose to be out and comfortable around me.

"I should name you," I said, stroking the creature with the horn. As I thought up ideas, a sudden memory hit me like a blast of wind: The very first toy we got Lili was a little rag doll we bought from the market. But something about its scraggly material collected every bit of dust around it, turning it into a different color every day. I would always complain about this, until eventually Lili started referring to the toy as 'Dusty,' also making it one of her first words. Edgar thought this was hilarious and never let up about it, even after we were forced to get rid of the toy and give her a better, non-dusty one.

"Dusty," I dubbed this creature.

A couple days later, I was riding her again, and we passed the well. I couldn't help but stiffen, and she slowed to a stop. Very gently, I tugged one of the spikes protruding from her head in the direction of the well, and we climbed inside. I collected the sack and all the items in it. And I held Colette's body, cradling her, tears streaming down. I laid her over Dusty's back. I put the tips of all my fingers together against my lips to make an eating gesture. Like the past couple of times, Dusty understood and accepted, going down on all fours and then leading me towards the woods where the berries were; I sat behind her and kept her steady the whole time.

Once we were there, I brought her into the meadow, dug with a spade from inside the sack, and finally buried her.

I mounted Dusty once more, leading her to the buildings near the castle, and going inside the one I had last seen Odysa. The smell was terrible, flies were buzzing. Dusty hopped a bit and dashed towards her, but I ran into her side view and slapped my thigh rapidly, calling her back to me. She skidded to a stop, looking from my shaking head to Odysa and then her tail drooped and dragged on the floor as she begrudgingly went to my side. I laid her over her back and brought her to the meadow, laying her to rest beside Colette. I plucked flowers from the meadow and laid them on top of both of their graves.

I spent every day of the next couple of weeks burying every single body in the smithy. I stared at Dusty, dug at the dirt with my hands and then made a digging motion. She caught on and began digging for me, the others mimicking her.

Once, Dusty glanced up abruptly and I swiveled my head in the direction of her gaze, my hopes soaring high for no reason at all. But it was nothing more than a deer. She glanced at me, as if to ask me for approval. I nodded and pointed and with that, she slashed the deer with her claws, bringing it down swiftly. She dragged the body behind a tighter cluster of trees, where she easily blended in and the shadows shielded her and the others who came close. There, she tore the gaps open wider, her tongue slipping inside and scooping out a couple guts, leaving when she was done to allow the others to go in and take their share. They all took turns, some even splitting their take with others, making efficient use of the creature's innards.

When the last person was finally buried, I just sat down and leaned against Dusty, the others fading into the landscape as they sat and moved about.

I could have spent the rest of my days here. Or I could have tried for another kingdom. I mean, Colette had to have been right that there were other people out there, but they were probably far from here now. There was no sign of any other form of life and I had been all over Orienne. But the way some of the buildings were boarded up and others ransacked—there was life here at some point, perhaps early on. It didn't matter where they were now; just that they *were* out there.

What if I tried to find them? It seemed an impossible task, but more and more impossibilities were becoming my reality each day.

However, if I did leave… I wouldn't be able to stop the creatures from harming anyone else that Commander Ingrith sacrificed to them. There hadn't been any lately, but I couldn't live with myself if there was another round of human souls brutally snatched away at the hands of creatures that might have listened to me if I asked them not to.

The best thing to do was to just stay here. Perhaps if more people were sent out, I could keep them safe from the creatures.

Perhaps I could teach them how to live with them and we could rebuild the kingdom together.

But then I thought about Colette and Odysa and Rowena and Edgar and Liliana and everyone in there at the moment. I thought about how long they had been trapped inside and how much longer they might still be trapped inside. It was not fair for me to be out here, safe and free, while everyone else was still in there, living a life of confinement and monotony and nothingness.

Not to mention I didn't know if I could go any longer without another human being to talk to. Without my child and husband to hold.

I realized something. This whole time, I had been wondering what was the best way possible to live my life to make Colette's sacrifice worth it, but the thing was the sacrifice would be worth it either way. The sacrifice had not been made with certain conditions; the only condition was life. Now, I got to do what I believed would make it meaningful to fulfill the value that she extrinsically put on my life.

Colette had told me to consider whether or not the slimmest sliver of a chance was worth risking everything. I stroked Dusty's head and smiled as I decided *Yes*. Yes, it was worth it. It always had been and always would be.

***

Commander Ingrith and all the other guards have frozen in place, their bulging eyes on me.

The last thing I wanted was for anyone to get hurt. I only wanted the creatures to be a threat tactic and security measure.

"They are not to be feared," I pronounce the words. "I am not here to attack or harm. I just want everyone to be free and together." I take a step closer, Dusty stepping with me. "Where are the men and children?"

Ingrith's face twists up. *How dare you*, it yells at me without saying anything. She throws her arm forward like it's a spear, and every arrow is flung, every guard now charging forward in spite of it all. The arrows bounce off of the creatures' armor-like scales, and they knock every approaching guard down to the ground.

They open their mouths into what must be terrible screams, for every single person in sight scrunches their face up and covers their ears as much as possible. Some fall to their knees, compressing their hands as hard against both sides of their head as they can.

I pat Dusty's neck, and we walk through the broken array of guards, no longer a rigid and aggressive formation but disconnected flecks of snow sprinkled across the sky.

Anice slides in front of me, covering her eyes and squinting. "Freya," her lips form. "North wing."

My eyes harden over her and before I know it my fist has flown against her cheek. Being the non-confrontational, peaceseeker that I have always been, I had never once in my life raised my hand against another being, let alone knocked my fist against them with everything inside me. Yet here I am now, my fist throbbing, Anice knocked down to the floor, spitting out blood. "That's for Odysa," I say.

Then, I head through the forbidden halls in that direction, no one stopping me, surrounded by serene waves of large creatures that flow steadily all around me.

I lead them through the castle, a shiver running down my spine as I pass the cellar we were all kept in, and go down the stairs, everything getting dimmer and dimmer.

There are a few guards standing in the middle of the empty corridor—men. They turn pale when they spot me and all the creatures around me. In the next moment, they spin around and bolt in the other direction. I feel Dusty hop a bit, the excitement spreading through the other creatures. I hold her back and her steps steady again, the others calming as well.

The guards open a set of doors and rush inside. I pat Dusty and she slides against the doors, keeping it open. The guards instantly drop everything and retreat into the room as Dusty shoves the doors wide open. I walk in with the rest of the creatures.

There are round tables all around, men sitting about and eating. Once they catch sight of us, they jump to their feet, tripping over themselves and the tables to get to the far end of the room, knocking over plates and chairs and each other. Everyone squeezes together as far away as possible, the guards gulping harshly as they step forward with their weapons up.

I put my hands in the air as a couple arrows fling towards us. I flinch, covering myself instinctively, but just like earlier, they merely bounce off the creatures' thick hides, sending them back towards the men. Two guards race towards us with their swords up, all the others staying back. The creatures bump them with their heads, knocking them to the ground. One of them gapes and scoots back frantically; the other grits his teeth and continues swinging his sword even when he is down.

The creature lifts his claws up to slash at him, but Dusty opens her mouth, a vibration making the floor tremble. This creature pauses mid-movement and slowly sets his leg down. His tail wraps around the knight's arm, halting his swinging abruptly, and then flings him to the other side of the room where the rest of the men are.

I take a look at the spectacle before me. It is so strange seeing men again; they almost seem to belong to another species at this point. And to see them all cowering before me in fright.

My heart twists. "Please do not fear," I say. "You are all safe. The creatures that threatened us will no longer harm us."

They gawk, eyes bulging, tears in their eyes, some of them gripping one another—all of them frozen in place. I do not feel any of their horror-stricken hearts ease.

"Follow me if you wish to see your families and be free," I say.

No one moves. Everyone just continues to stare as if they are watching a ghost.

Then, one man stands up.

He is tall with shaded olive skin, a pointy nose, and slick black hair. There are creases along his forehead and soft crinkles trickling off the rims of his velvety brown eyes. His cheeks are a bit sunken in. He has lost much muscle over the years.

I can hardly believe it's him.

He walks towards me, staggering as he practically drags his feet forward, immobilized by disbelief. He stands right before me, gaping at me the way one would at a phantom, crying at me the way one would at a pocket of escaped paradise that somehow fell into their world.

I don't realize I'm doing the same thing until I smile at him and the smile seems to break my numbed face like an ax through a sheet of ice. And with that, it is like all of our senses are restored. We don't waste another second; in our next breath, we are in each other's arms.

We hold each other tightly, as if each second can make up for a year in lost time. But in this moment, all the years just come rushing back and it's as if we never spent a moment apart.

When we pull away, our hands stay interlocked.

"Where are the children?" I call out as the guards start to get closer on all sides. Edgar stands back and watches me, both dumbfounded and awe-struck.

The guards grab at any man they can and yank them back or plummet them to the floor. They lift their swords and swing at the creatures even after seeing how futile this has been thus far. The creatures merely growl and bump into them or fling their tails into their armor, which is enough to send them crashing back.

I pat Dusty. She looks at me, awaiting directions. I move my open palms outward from my lips to the open air on either side of my head, slightly turning my hands. Then, I point at the guards.

She trots towards the nearest guard. He puts his sword up but she just knocks it away with one bump of her sturdy muzzle. As he trips over his feet, she steps over him and roars in his face. Every single person in the room stops what they are doing to cover their ears, some even dropping to the ground. Edgar's hand slips away from mine as he protects himself as well.

The guard's face twists and his body rolls from side to side. Blood drizzles down from his ears, staining his palm and wrist.

I gasp. What have I done!

I pat my lap frantically, Dusty stepping off of him as I rush towards him, bending down with an outstretched arm. His tightened face does not loosen and he serves me a cold glare as he scoots away. His lips move about around his gritted teeth, "They're in the east wing, probably down in the dungeons at this time."

I turn to Edgar to verify this, and he gives me the sign for dungeons as he picks up the guard's sword.

I turn the creatures around, waving for everyone to follow suit, Edgar echoing my gestures. Their faces are tattered with confusion and uncertainty. Nevertheless, next thing we know, there is a crowd behind us, squeezing into the circle bordered by the creatures who fend the guards off and force them back.

I look at Edgar. "You still remember my language?" I sign.

"I practiced when I could. Just in case," he signs back. He glances at all the people around us, and at all the creatures. "Who would have thought…?"

"I'm the last person who would have." Even now, it doesn't feel real. It feels like a ridiculous fairy tale. The most ridiculous part of it being *me.* Me, of all people.

Guards—both men and women—barricade the entrance to the dungeons, their weapons raised. Ingrith must have already rushed here to warn them. One man and woman guard stand at the very front of all the forces. "Don't," the man enunciates, his Adam's apple bobbing and eyes nervously darting from creature to creature. I can feel the fear that trickles out of all of the guards like water from an overfilled goblet.

I step forward, Dusty and the others pushing the guards to the side.

The man waves his hand and quickly sends everyone dispersing to the sides, stepping aside to let all of us through. The woman guard steps forward and pulls a key out. It bounces around in her hand, not letting her stick it into the lock. I set a hand over hers, trying to send her any comfort I can. She tenses up, looking at the creatures and then at me before finally opening the door successfully.

We enter the dungeons, a series of cell blocks furnished with beds and tables, all of which are wide open and illuminated by lit torches and barred windows.

But that is not what any of us are focused on.

Children bustle about the hallways and the cells, sitting on beds and talking, leaning against walls, singing soft songs. Most of them are adolescents, some on the edge of young adulthood, and none of them are any younger than five.

But they are all here.

They slowly stop what they are doing and examine us the same way we are examining them, completely dumfounded and awe-struck.

Some of the men bump past me, yelling names and running into this new population, and next thing I know, I am surrounded in a swirl of happy reunions.

Edgar takes my hand, his mouth moving in a repeating shout. "Lili!" I join in on calling as we squeeze our way past people.

We go through each cell, down every hallway, around corner after corner, squeezing through the claustrophobic storm of people. A knot forms in the pit of my stomach, getting tighter and tighter with every moment that drifts by with Liliana nowhere to be seen.

Edgar tugs my arm back, calling my eyes to his. They are soft and sorrowful, treading towards that painful area I want no part in, the one that tells me to brace myself in case—

No, this cannot be it. We are so close to everything I ever wanted. I refuse to believe Lili is not here somewhere.

Just then, I spot a young girl hiding timidly in the corner. Hope crawls back into me, gripping my heart and raising it up from the ground where it had sunken. I pat Edgar frantically, and we both head over there.

"Lili?" I gasp out.

The child shyly steps forward, another little girl next to her.

Her skin tone seems to have paled over the years but it is still a perfect mixture of Edgar's and my rich and soft complexions. She has my round nose and full cheeks and Edgar's smooth black hair. And my, has she grown—she's up to my shoulder now rather than just barely at my elbow.

This is her. This is actually her.

My head spins and heart twirls, the rest of me doing its best to keep myself from snatching her up off the ground and spinning her around in the air.

But her eyes do not gleam with elation—rather, with confusion and wariness.

I bend down. "I'm your mother, dearie. And he's your father."

She seems to strain her brain, as if bringing back a memory that has long since slipped away. "Mom?"

I nod, a tear running down. I lift my wrist up, displaying the lace. Lili looks at her own wrist, tracing her finger over her lace—it is still there. After all this time, it is still there.

The corners of her lips raise, and I remember she also has Edgar's bright smile. I lean over and we hug each other tightly. Edgar wraps his arms around us both, all of us twitching from the tears that escape out of us.

I could stay in this embrace for forever. If I could stretch this moment out to eternity, I would in a heartbeat.

I don't even care what happens next. Perhaps that sounds ignorant or overly bold, but it's the genuine truth. Being able to hold my family again was all I wanted and now I finally have them. No matter what happens next, this moment here, this moment of love and purity and warmth that prevailed through all the tumultuous storms like a dove through the skies of a battlefield—this moment has made it all worth it and will make whatever shards of darkness that await us worth it.

We finally let go, but our bodies stay pressed into one another, Edgar's arm around my waist and on Lili's shoulder. I sniffle, my heart so full it could burst.

Lili looks at a little girl besides us, who says something to her.

"She said, 'I told you, you had a mom, too,'" Edgar signs to me.

I pat the little girl's head, who is watching us closely. "What's your name, sweetheart?"

"Eve."

"Eve, we will find your mommy as well, alright? That is our next stop." They're all probably having dinner right about now. I can just envision the slumpy pile of food, the wide room of scattered wooden tables and overlapping conversations.

"Okay." She shrugs indifferently, as if that is the last thing she is worried about. "I don't think she's lost, though."

"Not lost?"

"I see her all the time."

My brows furrow, not quite sure what to make of that. Edgar taps my shoulder, bringing me to the present, to more pressing matters.

I turn to the guards, who have been kept back by the creatures and forced to simply watch all of this with no chance of moving forward. I see Commander Ingrith, a stern male guard, and the two male and female guards who were guarding the entrance to the dungeons.

"It's over," I call out. "Please, let us just talk through all of this. We no longer have to be afraid of the outside. We can rebuild

Orienne from out there—or even inside the castle if that is what is preferred."

All the movements from both guards and villagers have steadied to soft exchanges of glances, shuffling of feet, shifting eyes. I see annoyance, frustration, fear, bewilderment, distrust, belittlement, but also flecks of hope.

Then, a surge of energy courses through everyone like a blaze of lightning, and people are suddenly throwing things at me and yelling. Guards and villagers alike.

Edgar pulls me down, and we all duck behind Dusty. I catch the brunt of some of their open-mouthed yells: "Demon." "Temptress." It seems some of them must be convinced I am some sort of monster as well, or someone who wants to hold their hands and walk them to their demise.

"Stop!" I cry out, but by now it is useless. It doesn't matter who started the chaos; for even if the guards are taking the most advantage of it now, everyone here has been ensnared by it like prey. Arrows are flying about. Swords are lurching forwards. Guards are ripping people apart from one another. Villagers are fist-fighting guards and creatures.

The creatures growl and snap with both their fangs and their claws, striking people down bloodily. I stroke Dusty, striking the side of my hand against my palm and shaking my head. She lifts her head and mouth in the air, the creatures looking up for a moment before they quickly go back to simply using their tails to whip people back.

Edgar taps my arm. "We must go," he signs.

With his arm around me, I take Lili's hand. Her friend, who is only up to her shoulder, stares at us with wide eyes glossed with terror. I grab her hand as well.

We run up the stairs, into the light, Lili and Eve rubbing their eyes. "Come now, dears," I tell them as we continue running forward.

We come across other guards in the hallways, and people and creatures from down below begin splurging out behind and around us. We duck and dodge as much as we can.

Three male guards stand in front of us, and Dusty crashes into them, sending them to the floor. She picks one of them up by his ankle using her tail and throws him into the wall. She starts towards the second one, who slashes his sword about carelessly yet menacingly, one of his reckless strokes scraping across her scale-less shoulder and making her freeze in place, pained.

Meanwhile, the third one picks himself up and rushes towards us with his sword. My heart drops as I instinctively shove Lili and Eve behind me, while Edgar jumps towards him with the sword, the blades crossing over one another. The guard flicks his sword, quickly disarming him. The guard smashes the butt of his sword into Edgar's stomach, cutting his breath in half, and then hooks his leg around Edgar's, sending him tripping onto his face as the guard claims the fallen sword as his.

Edgar rolls about wildly, narrowly avoiding the his double stabs, the guard's face embroiled with concentration and fervor. Dumb and uncertain and starkly aware of my poor fighting skills and questionable survival instincts, I get ready to lunge at the guard from behind when someone else tackles me down first.

I rub my head to see it is Commander Ingrith standing above me. I shouldn't be surprised.

Lili is hugging Eve tightly, both of them weeping harshly. "Go!" I tell them, waving my hand frantically to the side. Ingrith whirls towards them, and I impetuously grab her ankle and pull her back, making her nearly trip.

She curls her lip and stomps on my face, sending me back down.

I clutch my bruised cheek. "Please, madam. There's no more use in fighting. Let's stand strong together."

She points her sword at my neck. "You can read lips, can't you, Freya?" she says.

I nod.

"Good, for I want you to thoroughly understand how much ruin you brought upon us. How much hard work you overturned in the course of a day."

I prop myself up on my elbows.

"As even you must know, Queen Hildegard summoned everyone here after people started getting killed off by these monsters with none of our conventional weapons working against them. She wanted to keep everyone safe while buying time to figure out what they were and how to combat them. That first night, she had us divide everyone for organizational purposes and collect their belongings to avoid any severe infighting in the meantime, for she knew how riled that many people, all of diverse statuses and backgrounds, could get in a small space.

"Of course, there were some who didn't obey the executive order and did not show up. That night, we watched them get ripped apart and parceled among the monsters from a window. There was nothing we could have done to save them. Yet something about this sight snapped something inside Queen Hildegard, and she was not quite the same afterwards. She lost herself, fell into a bit of a trance in which all she could do was wander aimlessly, dissociated from all reality, no matter what we did.

"All the while, the creatures tried to break in every day without rest. We barricaded the doors and windows as best as we could, keeping everyone in their designated sections as we focused our attention on working tirelessly to formulate a plan of action in an unprecedented time, no protocol or official ruler to guide us. No one to turn to, no one to reach out to, even as a desperate last resort. We were all that was left; it was all on us. People were getting restless, and I could feel the tensions starting to rise. I knew if we lost control inside, we would be done for.

"One day, a couple monsters managed to break through a side door, near where the children were being kept and they slaughtered a few of them—and Queen Hildegard. They just killed them and left, dragging their bodies out with them." Her knuckles clench up, turning white. "At the time, the guard that had been keeping supervision decided to implement a laid-back structure—and that was how those children and the queen slipped out into danger.

"But the creatures stopped trying to break in for a while. And that's when I knew what we needed to do."

"Sacrifices," I fill in.

"It was the only way to keep them appeased, at least temporarily," she explains. "There was much skepticism among my guards, especially the incompetent and ignorant ones. The same guard who had let the children and Queen Hildegard slip under his watch asked me what would happen when we ran out of people to sacrifice. I tried to get him and all the other guards to understand—we were all trapped in here. There was no way to fight these creatures, and if there was, we weren't going to find it anytime soon. None of us were going to live a very long life. Hence, all this was just being done to make Orienne last for as long as possible, to prolong a very soon death sentence.

"Still, he insisted there had to be another way. He and some others attempted to go outside and find this way—they were killed almost instantly.

"I didn't get much opposition from my people after that, for most were wise enough to understand by then. It was you villagers that presented a problem, asking all the questions that I did not have the answers to. I knew there was no way any of you would possibly possess the maturity to understand the necessity of my actions, no way any of you would be selfless enough to agree to what was being done for the greater good of us all. It would only work if you were all separate and divided up, dispersed and dependent. Otherwise, no one would listen, and Orienne would fall right then and there. People would go berserk." She gestures to me. "Case in point." I cringe. "We had to shepherd our sheep."

"You forced children to their deaths?" I croak.

"We picked the elderly and sick first from the male and female populations, sacrificing a few every month. Because the woman population was larger, we had to pick from our section more. But we have not subjected any children to those monsters. We are trying to keep them alive as long as we can. That is all I was ever trying to do."

"What were you going to do once you ran out of people? Surely you weren't planning on having the children on their own to fend for themselves. Were you going to stop when only you and your knights remained?"

"I was just trying to bide our time. I thought they might leave, or some miracle might find its way to us." She sighs. "Nothing about this was ever ideal, Freya. I was only ever doing what had to be done to protect and uphold what was left of the kingdom. It was far from an easy task, but I did everything I could to fulfill it. I was Queen Hildegard's most faithful servant; *I* continued her legacy. And I did a damn good job that I ought to be commemorated for."

Tears fall down my eyes as I let all of this sink in, my lip quivering.

They truly had been killing us off then. I had already speculated all this long ago, but to have it dictated to me like this is a whole other thing. Honestly, I think we all knew this, one way or another—How could we not after being torn away from our families and seeing our numbers diminish insidiously? — but we just pretended not to.

Is it possible that I truly did ruin the only chance any of us had? That Commander Ingrith had been in the right all along, and I had just yanked all of our death sentences years closer?

I glance at Edgar. The guard slams both swords into the floor, one of them getting stuck and refusing to come up with his pull. Edgar takes this chance to slide underneath him and tackle him from behind, making the guard hobble and giving Edgar the chance to pull the stuck sword out himself. Finally giving him a fighting chance.

I don't see Lili anywhere, but I just know in my heart that she is safe. For we also gave *her* the fighting chance she needed.

"Queen Hildegard would be proud of you. How you've adapted and evolved," I say, rising to my feet. "You just need to do it one more time. Perhaps this all did start off with you doing what you believed you had to, but there is an even better way. The creatures can listen to us, and we can all stand together as one, no one better or lesser or alone. No more blood has to be shed."

She looks me up and down, and for the first time ever her eyes soften. She thinks some more, lowering her sword. "You're right. No more blood has to be shed," she says contemplatively, eyes darting about as if to keep up with her racing thoughts. Then, her brows furrow. "No more after yours." She lifts her sword up to lurch it forward with gusto, leaving me to just helplessly cover myself with my arms, when I see Dusty's figure leaping onto her from behind.

But Ingrith gasps and slides out of the way just in time, so Dusty's body crashes into me instead, bringing me back down hard to the floor.

She stands above me with her legs on all sides of me, still standing firmly. Real fear starts to creep into me.

She lifts one leg up, her claws out and ready to gash apart my insides with one deadly hit, then pauses as she thankfully realizes it is me.

But a fraction of a second later, her mouth is wide open in a screech.

Edgar is standing next to her, pushing a sword into one of her scale-less spots with all his strength. He plunges deep through her thick hide so that only the handle of the sword is poking out now.

"Edgar, no!" I yell. He didn't see what just happened. All he saw was a beast attacking and about to kill me after he somehow miraculously made it away from the guard.

A river of black blood pours out of her from under the sword. She stumbles off of me and towards Edgar, swiping at him sporadically with her claws, his blood splattering in all directions.

"Dusty, stop! Please!" I slap my thigh, my whole body shaking, tears racing down both my eyes and making my face as wet as if I had been dunked in a river.

Dusty turns her head away from Edgar and towards me. I tap the side of my hand over my palm, knowing she will understand and listen and step off of my husband who just made a terrible, terrible mistake.

But she just turns back to him and continues slashing him apart.

That's when it dawns on me.

This whole time I thought I was commanding her, but she was simply entertaining me the way a host accommodates a guest. My 'orders' were never orders but requests that she had been obliging to out of courtesy and kinship. And now I have finally made a request that she does not want to fulfill.

Desperate and frantic, I grab the spikes around her head and pull them, leaning my whole body back to try to tug her off the love of my life. A rapid vibration runs through her, yet she stays in place, slicing and clawing. She hits me with her tail, making me double over and stumble backwards, out of her way.

There's only one more thing left to do.

I clench my fist up and pound it against her bad eye. She freezes, her body stiffening and striking out, her mouth widening even further. I cringe, a part of me wanting to scramble to apologize and soothe her pain away in spite of everything.

Dusty moves away from Edgar and faces me. Edgar is not moving.

His arms that used to sway me when we danced are not moving. His chest that used to breathe life into me is not moving. His eyes that used to overflow with compassion and twinkle with joy when they settled over Lilianna and me are not moving.

Dusty gazes at me, looking me up and down and baring her teeth. With tears falling out, I back away as she stalks closer and closer, her tongue flickering out.

Then, she snaps her enormous jaws around me. I feel the pain of a thousand daggers inserted through the entire trunk of my neck, but only for a fraction of a second before they snap and crush my bones.

I rub my wrists and ankles, finally free from the rope, having spent the past hour or so biting at the knot with my teeth—after shaking the gag off—in a way that made my whole mouth sore and made everyone look at me, clearly thinking, *She really has lost her mind.*

Now, they have a different look in their eyes. I go to each of the other six women here, removing their gags and working to undo their bounds as well.

"Hello? Guard?" the only other woman around my age repeats over and over again like a broken music box.

Leaning against the door, I hear nothing but ominous screeches—but not like the ringing we used to hear all the time. These are loud enough to make the ground rumble and are so close I back away from the door. The sounds of people screaming and running are sprinkled generously in there.

Out of the corner of my eye, I see a giant spider the height of the ceiling, covered with bushels of prickly, thorn-like hairs, crawl down the side of the wall. The tapping of its eight legs against the floor as it gets closer to me create little echoes through the earth—or is that from the chaos outside?

I close my eyes and take a deep breath. Did it have to show up now, of all times?

The other women here are already cringing and looking about with fear in their eyes, and following my gaze just further warps this fear. I look away from the spider, knowing better than to pay my uncontrollable imagination any mind now.

"Are the guards really not there?" one of the older women, a lady with tan skin and wavy grey hair up to her shoulders, asks.

"It seems like they are a bit preoccupied," I answer, my stomach twisting. Biting my lip, I pull out the hairpin in my hair and stab it into the lock, twisting it around in all directions. I've never picked a lock before, if you can't tell. I've also never been locked in a room with people that were going to be forced out of the castle only for who-knows-what to be happening outside now. We really are just puppets being dragged from one shadowy play to another.

"Allow me," the woman says. I move aside and let her take over. With just a couple swirls of the hairpin, there's a click. "My grandchildren had a habit of accidentally locking themselves in my closet." She tries for the handle, and it is loose. She slowly cracks it open, just barely, and peeks outside. Almost instantaneously, she gasps and shuts the door right back.

"What is it?" I ask, looking out.

I see people running and screaming in scattered and aimless directions, tripping over one another, horror-stricken like never before, a strange and invisible course of energy ripping through them. But when the people fall down, the movement of this energy seems to settle and I see it is not a vague force crashing through the people outside. They are humongous, hellish monsters.

I close the door. This has to be another one of my hallucinations. They usually are not nearly as intricate and complex as this, but perhaps they've exacerbated without me realizing.

Besides, the only other alternative would be that this is all actually happening. The monsters outside actually are real and we actually are in more danger than we ever could have imagined.

I look at the woman. "What is your name?"

"Estrilda."

"Estrilda," I repeat, "what did you see?"

Her eyebrows furrow questioningly. "What might as well have been a war!" I wait. "A war against demon-like beasts." There it is.

I tense up. So, it is true then…

Unless *this* woman is unreal.

I know I'm reaching now, but I cannot help it.

I place a hand on her shoulder. The bafflement twists her face even tighter.

I don't know whether to be relieved or even more terrified at this confirmation. My hand starts to tremble against her shoulder. I drop it back to my side. "Alright," I say. "May I ask what everyone's name is?"

One of the twins, a stout woman with mono-lid eyes and short silver hair, scoffs. "Is that really a priority right now?"

"I figure we are all on the brink of death, so we might as well acquaint ourselves."

"The brink of—?"

"I'm Dhea," a woman rolls her wheelchair forward and puts a hand in the air to interrupt her. She has a curved nose, brown skin, and a wrinkled and sweet face.

"Hattie," the petite lady standing beside Dhea says. Her hunched back makes her lean over on her cane, and she has small, circular spectacles framing her diamond-blue eyes.

"Clarisse," the only other young woman says, her finger tapping anxiously against her thigh. She has copper hair tied back in a braid with freckles dotting her face.

The short-haired twin sighs impatiently, speeding through her introduction. "I'm Maud, and that's my sister, Glinna." She points at the woman next to her, who is playing with the ends of her long hair. They are almost exact replicas of one another, except for the hair. "Can you tell us what you saw now?"

"Alright," I say, "the monsters seemed to have breached the castle. I'll check again, and when it seems to be somewhat safe, we shall make a run for it."

The others exchange glances. Clarisse steps forward. "You must live up to your moniker if you truly believe going out there is a good idea."

I suppose snide comments like that ought to be nothing more than dust to brush off my shoulders after a lifetime of constantly hearing them, especially during my worst breakdowns. I suppose they should be nothing new to me after hearing much worse from my own parents before they abandoned me at a young age to fend for myself. But they will never be anything less than sharp stabs that rip me apart from the inside out.

I sigh. "Look, the way I see it, Clarisse, we have two choices. We either remain in here, or we use this as a distraction to get out. The guards were planning on feeding us to them after all, so we are just as dead if we stay."

"Yes, but to go out there? Into what has become a battleground?" She leans in, dropping her voice to a whisper. "Stringing along five people who hardly know their own names?"

"I'm with Clarisse here. How am I supposed to trust you?" Maud pipes in.

You would not be with her if you had heard everything she said, I think. "Look, you are free to do whatever you wish. I'm simply stating what *I'm* about to do." They both recoil, clearly not happy but also starkly aware of our lack of options.

"Does anyone know the way out of here?" I ask.

"Dhea, weren't you a maid here?" Hattie taps the end of her cane against the wheel of her friend's chair.

"Yes, I was. I may not have the best memory, but I have every nook and cranny of this place seared into my brain."

"Wonderful," I say. "I also have to find my friend."

"Let's focus on surviving first," Clarisse remarks.

"Of course," I answer, though I cannot say for sure which task I am prioritizing first.

It seems to have quieted a bit outside. Just ever so slightly, and the roaring seems distant now. I peek out again. There are just a couple people rushing past now, and I don't see any of the creatures.

"It's time," I announce, and I open the door the rest of the way out, stepping into this other world, my heartbeat ringing in my ears with these couple of steps.

I hold the door for them and they shuffle out with trepidation. Dhea rolls her wheelchair out. Hattie is close beside her, one hand leaning against her chair, her steps uncertain and subtly wobbly. Maud guides her sister out gently, who looks around from side to side but comes along indifferently. Estrilda is the last one out, scanning the room one last time before nodding at me to let the door go.

"Which way, Dhea?" Hattie asks. Dhea squints her eyes, her forehead wrinkling.

"Great," Clarisse grumbles. "It's not like we're out in the open or anything."

Estrilda shoots her a glare that makes her blush and look down. Dhea's eyes light up. "This way," she points.

I hurry in that direction, a frantic bounce catapulting my steps. "How long are we continuing in this…?" I turn and realize they are still on the other side of the hallway. I sigh and return to them, doing my best to quiet the bubbling in my chest with patience. I whip my head back and forth, part of me desperately searching for Sidonie, the other just waiting for one of the monsters to burst out.

"Where are we going?" Glinna asks her sister, her forehead scrunched up. "We'll be late to the feast."

"We're headed to the feast," Maud tells her. "Just be quiet and let me handle this."

A sudden commotion originates from behind us. My heart jumps to my mouth before I realize it is just a group of people running—women and *men* and I swear I see children mixed among them. We stop in place, gawking.

"Hurry and follow us to the grand entrance!" one of the men yells.

Clarisse is the first to shake herself off, knowing any questions can be reserved for later. She starts to pick up speed, boosting herself in front of all of us before she slows down, throwing her head back at us. She bites her lip, guilt seeming to drown her and tear her in two. I recognize that look.

"It's alright," I tell her. "Truly."

She nods. "Make it out of here," she says as she runs to join the others.

"You ought to go as well. Get out of here faster," Estrilda says gently. The tenderness in her eyes is mingled with surefire determination and willpower, all of which overpower any fear and uncertainty that exists in her. I look at the four other women here, and they have the same fire in all of their eyes.

I shake my head. "We're in this together."

Just then, the demonic beasts run out from the side hallway that intersects with ours. Estrilda grips my arm, as if to yank me back, and we all freeze to watch the monsters run into the center and effectively block our way.

"There is another way out," Dhea says with a hesitant edge, waving her hand and backing us into another hallway. "It's a bit longer and more round-about, though. And it poses its own challenge." She leads us before a long series of descending steps.

We all eye Dhea's wheelchair. Dhea winces, and Maud opens her mouth to say something. But without wasting another breath, Hattie steps behind her and grips onto the handles, handing Dhea her cane to hold. With that, I move to stand at the front of the wheelchair and hold onto the edges of the seat.

Dhea relaxes, an unspoken gratitude on her face, and she nods.

Estrilda gives us one last worried glance before she goes before us, using both hands to grapple tightly onto the railing and guide her journey down. Maud and Glinna lean against each other and slowly go down each step.

"Are you alright?" I ask the three of them.

Estrilda nods, and Maud grumbles impatiently, "Yes, yes."

I'm about to roll my eyes when I catch Glinna smiling at me. Her eyes gleam with kindness. She is missing much of her upper teeth, making the smile seem even wider. "You are such a darling," she tells me. Something about the genuineness of her sweetness makes it hard not to smile back in spite of everything happening around us.

"Thank you," I say. I turn back to Dhea and Hattie. "Ready?"

"Well, I'm not ready to die," Dhea replies. Hattie smirks.

I smile and we begin our descent. Hattie carefully heaves Dhea's wheelchair down the first step, and I gently tug and resist from the front, keeping it steady. In this way, we all make our way down, pausing after each flight of stairs to take a breath.

Hattie looks at the rest of the panting women leaning against the end of the railing. "We are almost there," she tells them.

"Not quite," Dhea says, and Hattie shoots her a look. Dhea cringes, lifting her shoulders in a well-it's-true shrug.

"What's that?" Glinna asks curiously. We follow where her finger is pointing—to the five enormous creatures at the bottom of the stairs we are on top of. They camouflage so well with the castle walls they would disappear into them if not for the vigorous, aggressive manner they move in.

They surround three armored men, all taking part in ripping through them. Using their claws and teeth, they gash through their armor, ignoring their cries and the frantic waves of their weapons.

I watch dumbly as a couple peasants accidentally run into this, probably not spotting them at first. Once they do, they scream and run away, only for two of the monsters to leave the now unmoving knights to whip their tails at these peasants' ankles, gripping them and yanking them towards them. One monster roars in the person's face before digging in with its brutal claws. The other skips the formalities and sinks its teeth right in. They tear them apart carelessly, stuffing their ugly mouths inside them. The other three creatures lift their mouths out of the torn-up knights and walk away indifferently, presumably to spread their reign of terror. They move with no clear goal or desire, only to fill a bottomless pit of hunger and anger, as if there is nothing left to care about other than this.

My mouth drops as horror and anguish weaken my bones and muscles.

"You're going to die," a two-headed lady sings, creating an echoing harmony with her two voices—another regular hallucination of mine. She leans in closer to my ear. "You are all going to die."

"Marsily!" Estrilda shakes my shoulder, and I realize all the women have been calling my name for some time now.

"It's too late to back away now. We must go while they're still distracted," Maud states firmly, her hand over Glinna's eyes.

"Let go!" Glinna grumbles. Her sister drops her hand, rubbing her back gently until she calms down.

I nod weakly, and with the two-headed lady enlightening the background with her persistent song, we all go down the stairs. We keep a sharp eye on the monsters as they eat greedily with their backs to us, blood and guts splattered messily around them.

My foot settles on the floor under the last step, the others stepping beside me, the dancing flame of a torch on the wall that somehow still hasn't blown out making our shadows seem much larger than they actually are. There is nothing more than a couple steps' distance separating us from the feasting creatures. Dhea jerks her head to the left, and we all shuffle in that direction.

One of the monsters' nostrils flares, and its head whips towards us, making my heart just about stop. Its eyeless head turns towards its comrade, and they both abandon the corpses, their large strides making them just about fly towards us, as we all shriek. I lift my arms up in what I know will be a useless attempt to shield myself, realizing I will never see Sidonie again.

Then, a torch bounces off the monster's wide and sharp face before landing on the floor, the fire rapidly drawing a sharp line between them and us. The creatures cry out, stepping back and to the side, the one shaking its head about.

"Hurry!" Estrilda yells, wiggling her arm, which must be sore after throwing a heavy, flaming object. We waste no more time in rushing past them.

We've reached a part of the castle even more deeply submerged in chaos, bodies strewn about, both living and not. Among a couple of these bodies is one of the monsters—except this one is fallen over. Without stopping, I give it another look, just to ensure it is indeed dead. It turns out these creatures actually aren't eyeless—the eyes are just very small and blend into their bodies—unless this one is merely a special variant. Which is quite possible, considering it also is the only one I've seen with a large horn in the center of its head. Its eyes are foggy and vacant, and its mouth cracked open, tongue lolled out onto the floor. Black goo stains its shoulder and foreleg as if it was struck by the night sky.

My shoe sticks to the blood that taints the floor, making it take an ounce more energy to peel it off to step over dead bodies and keep moving. Turning my head back to the world before me, people bustle against us as they run ahead. Maud wobbles a bit from the bump, and I fling my hand out to support her.

Then, I spot Sidonie.

She is zigzagging across the hallway, tying tourniquets, bringing people to their feet, patting their shoulders, the ends of her braids bouncing off the back of her shoulder as she bumbles about. She bends down, ripping a strip of her dress off, which is already half its length and frilled jaggedly and unevenly at the end. She sits a guard up, asking—no demanding—something of her. What, I cannot tell among the noise and chaos; all I can see are the determined furrow of her eyebrows and the tense purse of her lips as she spits out what might as well be fire. The knight shakes her head and Sidonie heaves a sigh, a quick pause before she begins tying the piece of her dress around a bleeding cut on the knight's head. The knight gives her a double-take, as if astounded by her continued help. Though when she leans in and her lips move again, the guard hangs her head in shame.

My heart is fluttering, and it is impossible to contain myself any longer. "Sidonie!" I screech, my voice cracking.

A new energy lights up in her and she whirls in my direction. Her brows curve, tears filling her eyes instantly. Without saying another word, we run through all the violence surrounding us into each other's arms, hugging each other in an unspoken promise to never let the other go again.

"I was searching like hell for you," she sobs.

A bunch of things fall out of her pocket, landing between our feet. I wipe my eyes, and she sniffles as we break the hug.

"We better go," she says.

"I'm with five other women." I look behind me; they are quickly catching up to us now. Then, I drop to the floor to help her collect the couple of darts, bottles of medicines, and small, wrapped packages.

"What are these?" I ask.

"I discovered the guards' storage room. Turns out they have been hoarding all of our belongings there. They have an entire garden and extra kitchen hidden away!"

"They do?"

"And all this time, they were acting as if we only had *scraps* to go around," she grumbles. "Anyway, I grabbed some useful items."

I open up one of the soft objects, revealing a white pastry with icing on top. "Sweets?"

"Sustenance, of course."

It's been five years since we have even seen sweets, and holding this one now feels forbidden. I notice it is half-eaten. "Did you find it like that?" I tease.

"What was I supposed to do; *not* eat it?"

"You're probably the reason they kept this secret; it would have depleted within days if you had known." She laughs out loud.

"You must be Marsily's friend," Estrilda says.

"Yes, sorry for running off like that," I say. "I didn't mean to—"

"Words can wait. Let's keep moving," she says kindly.

"Wait," Sidonie says, and she looks around the entire area. There appears to no longer be anyone here but us and the dead bodies. "Alright, let's go."

"Which way, Dhea?" I ask, and she ushers us onward.

"Are you certain this is the way?" Sidonie asks, gesturing in the opposite direction where the blurry images of people's distant backsides can be spotted.

"This should be a clearer path," she answers. "We'll end up at the grand entrance, same as them."

She nods, then turns to me. "Have you seen Amira by any chance?"

"I'm sorry; I haven't seen your cousin anywhere. Perhaps she made it out before us."

Her brows twitch in distress. "I pray that's the case. She was in the privy at the time this all happened, and I've been up and down the castle searching for you two." She glances at all of us. "Let's all get out of here first, and then if need be, I'll return on my own to look for her."

"Don't be outrageous," Maud says. "We'll be lucky enough to make it out."

"I'll go with you," I assure her.

Tears make her eyes shine and she nods.

She clears her throat. "Do any of you know what's happening? Other than the fact that the monsters broke into the castle and the guards completely lost control? We were just having dinner when the guards began to look panicked and leave their posts. Someone must have managed to unlock the doors because then everyone poured out of there—but things quickly erupted into chaos as no one knew where to go or what to do. And then we saw the creatures…" She shudders. "I heard one woman led all the monsters in here, but that was from someone who was on the verge of bleeding out, so who knows?"

"Well, it seems that the guards have been less than truthful to us," I say.

"Clearly," she says with a biting edge to her voice. "The children and men have been alive this whole time, and merely kept in separate areas of the castle!"

"Not to mention, they tried to feed us to the monsters," Hattie pipes in.

"*What?!*" Sidonie cries out.

"That's what they do," Maud says.

"My goodness—"

Just at that moment, I start to hear a subtle ringing, but before I can make anything of it, a monster jumps out, having blended in perfectly against the wall, and slashes at me. Flinching, I instinctively turn to the side and stick my arm out as a shield, and the monster gashes my entire arm.

"No!" Sidonie yells, snatching the middle of its tail as it furls before her and yanking it. The creature swings its tail so she is catapulted off.

Meanwhile, I am just wobbling about, my vision blurry, and in the worst pain I've ever been in. The monster swings at me again with its claws but I somehow manage to duck. Before I can feel any sort of victory, however, my arm has been impaled by a hundred of its sword-like teeth. And all I can do is scream and uselessly pound on the top of its tightly-closed muzzle.

Hattie smacks the creature's head over and over with her cane. Sidonie stabs dart after dart into the hide of its cheek. Estrilda, Dhea, and Maud punch at it aggressively and vigorously.

Glinna stands back and away, her face in a confused and terrified knot. "Do I hit it?" she asks Maud.

"Yes! As hard as you can!" Maud exclaims, waving Glinna over. Glinna curls her fists and assists in pounding so they are all attacking it at once.

But the creature does not flinch. It just growls, the vibration running through my bones.

My other hand falls to my side, nothing left in me to keep fighting against it, while everyone else keeps on doing what they can to fight this beast.

Goodness, it would be better if they just left the creature alone and let it get on with killing me already. Weakly, I look at the face of the tortuous creature that is holding me hostage. Little dark circles on the center of its head twitch about, and I realize these are its eyes. So perhaps it's safe to assume they all truly do have eyes, then.

"Marsily!" Sidonie calls, watching me closely.

"Watch it," I mumble out as the creature lifts a claw up to swipe at all of them.

Sidonie steps to the side and dives onto the top of its leg, making the creature stumble, my arm jostled painfully in the process. "Get the eyes!" Sidonie cries out as she holds the leg tightly, the creature starting to lift its other claw up.

All the efforts are directed towards the two small black pupils, punching and striking them mercilessly. The creature drops its leg down and walks back in pain. It opens its mouth to let out a harsh screech, the fangs shifting slightly upward but not yet leaving the holes they've dug through my skin.

Finally, it falls down, the teeth tearing my arm off completely, and I topple to the floor. The creature stands up and runs off in pain, screeching and thrashing its head about.

Everyone hovers about me. The giant spider is back, snapping its pincers, the sound like a crack of thunder. The two-headed lady is no longer singing but pointing at me, doubled-over, the two heads cackling. My name is cried out by all of women I'm trying to escape with, but one specific source stands out among them all.

Sidonie ties a tourniquet around my arm; I hardly feel it. My whole body is tingly and distant. She holds my face, tears streaming wildly down hers. I turn my head towards what's left of my arm. It cuts off right under my shoulder, chipped bone sticking out of this bloody bundle of flesh and muscle. The rest of it lies, extended out and blood-splattered, beside my feet. I have seen some nightmare-fueling sights, but this one belongs to me more than any of the other ones, and something about that strikes too damn hard.

Well, if I needed any more confirmation of this being real, I certainly have it now.

The more I stare at all this, the more my head spins and the harsher my breaths escape my lungs. Then, it feels as if my entire body is about to explode and my heart gives in.

I think about the ways my hands have touched Marsily before—gently grazing her hair into a refined style, patting her arm in laughter, rubbing her back as she cries.

Now, I press my hands into her chest over and over again, watching her unconscious body rattle down and up and down and up. This is not how I want to hold her.

"Don't you dare," I hiss at her.

That's no way to talk to a patient, I can almost hear my father kindly scolding me.

The rims of my eyes burn hot. How come everyone I love feels so close yet so far?

My father was a doctor, one of the most excellent doctors in all of Orienne—I'd dare even say the best. When he died from the accident, we all knew that the only one who could have saved him was him.

I was going to be a doctor as well. My earliest memories are of sneaking around the hospital he worked at and watching him for hours (until I was ushered out in order to not scar my own innocent mind), so that I could imitate him at home alone in my room. He told me when I was older, he would let me apprentice him. But then life just had to steal him from me. He just had to slip and fall off that ladder while dusting off the walls of our home, head too cracked for any hope of repair, blood and bone splitting through the persisting traces of his constant smile. A wonderful father, a brilliant doctor, a good man—gone just like that.

My uncle and cousin were nothing but kind to me, yet even so, the fervor of my dream just died out. The clouds slowly dissipated from around my head to reveal that they were never clouds at all and I was never flying; they were nothing more than fog obscuring the real world and now I could see it all for what it truly was. And it was simply nothing special.

It seems that fog returned to me today, and only now is the cold, hard face of reality seeping into clarity once again.

Damn. I had so much nerve running around and playing doctor, didn't I? And now this is just reminding me that the game's over. I lost.

I look at my best friend, fading away before my very eyes, under my very grasp.

Goodness gracious, I lost.

Tears spill out of my eyes as whatever was holding me together just snaps in two. "WAKE THE HELL UP!" I screech in Marsily's face as I continue the compressions.

My eyes pop open and I take in the sharpest breath of air. I pant, feeling faint and dizzy.

Sidonie gasps in relief, more amazed than I am, tears spilling out. Her head falls onto my shoulder, dampening my dress; her hands find their way to my back, rubbing it as I breathe heavily. The spider and two-headed lady are nowhere to be seen. All the other women are still here, tightly compacted together, many of their hands and arms linked as one. After a moment or so, they all grab a part of me and help me rise to my feet.

"I stemmed the bleeding," Sidonie whispers, wiping her tears off her face. "Can you walk?"

I look at her, so damn happy to see her. "I think so."

With her arms supporting me, I lean on her and we all keep moving.

She gasps. "Behind the statue," she says, her voice tight, and we all huddle behind the large stone angel, the shadow of its wings sheltering us all as monsters stampede across, their cries piercing the air.

Out of nowhere, I feel a very strong tugging at my heart. "Sidonie," I say softly, barely loud enough to hear above the screeches and distant screams. She turns to me and I just pluck my lips on top of hers. I feel her jump the teensiest bit from shock, but in the next moment as I start to pull away, she pulls me back in with her lips, running her hand through my hair.

"Forgive me," I say when we let go. "I just-I brushed death far too many times today. I cannot let it happen again without having done that."

Sidonie strokes my cheek with her hand and smiles. "We will get through this." She turns to each of the women behind us. "We all will."

"Maud," Glinna says, pointing to the other angel statue right across from this one. I can hear crying behind it. Sidonie and I lean forward ever so slightly. I squint at it, and there I see it: two small children, cowered behind the angel, arms tightly wrapped around the other, weeping softly.

When the hallway is clear, Sidonie says, "I'll go check it out; would you all mind staying here for a quick moment?" She unhooks her arm around me, letting me lean against the statue. She looks around the hallway one more time, and then approaches them.

I see a shadow against the wall Sidonie is heading towards, one that shifts as if getting ready to pounce. A scream hops into my mouth and almost out of it before I see the giant pincers and the eight legs. I slap my palm over my mouth, trapping my scream and my terror inside me.

A monster, but not one of the ones we need to worry about.

"Are you alright?" Estrilda asks.

I want to just melt into the floor. It's almost like I can feel pieces of me dripping away, the fear and alarm making me feel weak and subhuman.

"I'll be back," I tell them as I go after Sidonie, stumbling and unsteady with nothing to hold onto.

Sidonie gives me and my arm a concerned and gently scolding look for making my way over here despite my condition. I crouch down next to her, in front of the two young girls. One is taller than the other so that she rests her chin on her head as they hug each other tightly.

"Hi, there," I say gently. "I'm Marsily, and this is Sidonie,"

The slightly taller girl wipes her almond-shaped eyes. "I'm Lili," she says.

The other girl has sandy skin and hair the color of hazelnuts. Timidly, she says, "I'm Eve."

"Are you waiting for someone?" I ask them.

They are silent. Lili looks down and says, "We were waiting for my mom and dad." I catch the hollowness in her voice.

"Perhaps your parents are outside," I offer. With that, Eve breaks down and sobs even harder.

Lili hugs her tighter. "Hers are not," she whispers.

My face heats up.

"Do either of you like games?" Sidonie asks all of a sudden.

Lili looks at her a bit bewildered, but nonetheless nods with Eve's head burrowed into her shoulder.

"Well, let's think of all of this as a game," she says. "A game where once we reach outside, we will have won. We are all actually rather close."

"What is out there?" Lili asks.

"That's the fun of the game—we do not know. It's a mystery. It could be sunken treasure or toys or… sweets," she says, beaming excitedly.

Lili cocks her head to the side. "What are sweets?" she asks. Meanwhile, Eve pulls away from Lili, intrigued.

Sidonie gives them each a pastry from her pocket. Usually, I would tell children not to accept food from strangers but I suppose it is fine for this instance.

Lili and Eve glance at the pastries hesitantly. "Go ahead," Sidonie encourages, and they slowly take it and bite into it. Lili's face lights up instantly, while Eve's is indifferent.

"But we have to hurry," Sidonie continues, "because there are other creatures who want to stop us from going out."

Lili and Eve look at each other, seeming to have a mental conversation, ending with the two of them nodding decidedly at one another as they turn back to us. Sidonie takes Lili's hand as she curls her other arm around my back again, and I take Eve's. "They're not going to hurt us," Lili says quietly.

"That's right, we won't," I affirm.

"I'm talking about the creatures," Lili says. Sidonie and I exchange glances.

We meet up with the rest of the women, and then waste no more time in getting going.

The end of my arm stings in a way that makes my entire body throb, and fatigue makes every one of my movements heavy. I notice the blood dripping down the floor from my arm.

"Are you alright?" Estrilda's voice pokes into my foggy mind.

I shake myself awake, only now realizing how close I got to passing over into unconsciousness again. "Y-Yes."

Sidonie rubs my back comfortingly.

"We're almost there," Dhea assures.

The sound of people gets louder and clearer until we make it to the main doors, where there is a huge crowd gathered, aggravated and pushing. At the very forefront are a series of guards with their weapons pointed, standing in front of the doors and not letting anyone get closer, led by Commander Ingrith. Some fight off monsters along the sidelines, only anxiously glanced at by the people here, as if that is only a secondary concern.

"This is not good for anyone," Estrilda mutters.

"The longer we stay crowded up like this, the easier it will be to pick us off," Maud grumbles.

"Follow Sir Valdis into the grand hall! You will be kept safe in there!" Ingrith yells.

A couple guards break away from the blockade and rush through the crowd, waving at them and leading them into the enormous room just a bit of a way from the doors. A fraction of the crowd tears itself off and follows them, while others shout back: "No!" "Let us through!" "If the monsters are in here, they cannot be out there!" "We are done listening to you!"

In response, Ingrith points at the monsters the guards are struggling to fight off, some of the guards already lying incapacitated on the floor. More come this way, just barely blocked off by the guards.

This sight is enough for a bigger chunk of the crowd to break off and run into the grand hall.

"Let's try for the servants' entrance," Dhea suggests.

"We have barricaded all the exits, so they are now impossible to break out of. Do not waste your time trying to disobey," Ingrith booms, as if she somehow picked up Dhea's singular voice of opposition in a sea of insanity.

The guard next to Ingrith turns to Ingrith, and I can swear the movement of his mouth says, "Are you certain of this?"

Ingrith says loudly, as if she wants all to hear, "When have I ever led any of us wrong?"

"They're coming!" I hear people scream, many whipping their heads towards the fight between the monsters and the guards, and dropping everything to run into the grand hall. With no other choice, we all follow them in that direction.

Eve points at the guard next to Ingrith. "He never let us play," she remarks quietly.

"She tried to kill my mom," Lili says, pointing at Ingrith.

I halt in my steps.

"Marsily!" Maud urges impatiently.

"If we go in there," I say, looking at each of them, "we are never going out again."

A new realization and hardness take over each one of their faces, even that of the children's, and we wordlessly come to a unanimous decision.

We are the only ones that stay in place, everyone else bumping past us to clear out of here, our grip on one another tightening to keep each of us steady in place. The crowd quickly diminishes to nothing but the guards, and together we all move closer to the doors.

Ingrith seethes upon sight of us. "Go help the others," she orders the rest of the guards, and they immediately rush towards the dozens of monsters off to the side and getting closer. She lifts her sword at us.

"Don't make us run you down," Maud hisses at her.

"I'll strike each of you before you can even think another thought on it," Ingrith says coolly.

We are in no state to fight. "Let us pass," I state firmly.

"You want to play this game, fine," Ingrith says. "I am not budging. And from where I am standing, I will have plenty of time to get away when the monsters tear you all down. I hope you make a wise choice."

I let all the words I would never dare to say except in hushed whispers or sneaky jabs come flowing out. "This is how you choose to command? In a world of fear and brokenness, you choose to press on the cracks keeping us apart? Just so you can enjoy the view from the top?"

"I always knew the lot of you were the most naïve things to walk the earth," she says, "but do you truly believe we would have lasted this long under anyone else but me?"

"Considering how much food you kept hidden out of reach *and* the fact you evidently have no issue feeding us to the monsters, yes, I do believe that, quite frankly," Sidonie replies sourly.

"Madam," one of the guards fighting off the monsters, a woman with thick, curly hair, breaks off to run next to Ingrith.

"Run them through," Ingrith orders her.

The guard's eyes scroll over every single one of us—what a sight we must be—the command seeming to rotate steadily around her head. Her eyes and her body harden and she takes a definitive step towards us, provoking all of us to tighten our hold around one another and step back. Eve hides her face in my dress, and Sidonie covers Lili's eyes.

Then, the guard spins and lunges at Ingrith.

I gasp, hardly able to believe it.

Ingrith blocks the guard's sword and disarms her. "How dare you?!" she barks, pointing her sword into her neck.

"Enough, madam," the guard says, her hands in the air. She tries to create space between them but Ingrith moves along with her, not allowing the smallest sliver of air. Maud, Estrilda, Dhea, and Hattie step towards them, but Ingrith swings her sword at them, forcing them to retreat a few steps back.

"I always knew you were weak," she spits out.

"This is no way to live," the guard pleads.

"And what would you have suggested?" Ingrith retorts condescendingly. "I did my best."

"No, Queen Hildegard did," the guard fires back. "*You* saw an opportunity and seized it." Ingrith's eyes widen and she glares harshly at her. "I didn't see it before, but now I do. Now I finally understand."

Ingrith presses in, the guard flinching away, and Ingrith nicks the side of her neck. The guard cries out and sinks to her knees, gripping her neck as blood pours out. Ingrith hovers over her, ready to crash her sword down.

Just then, Sidonie sticks her leg out and kicks the guard's fallen sword towards her. The guard snatches it off the floor and plunges it right into Ingrith's heart.

With that, Ingrith stops abruptly, her eyes wide open as if she cannot believe this. She plummets to the floor, her body rolling lifelessly.

Gritting her teeth, the guard yanks the sword out. "We must hurry," she tells us, letting go of her neck, just allowing it to flow freely now. "They'll only be able to hold off the monsters for so long, and the rest of them are bound to come down here any minute now."

She grabs the keys off of Ingrith's belt, holding a large silver one and letting the others jingle around her fingers. She extends it to us, and Estrilda takes hold of it. "Unlock the doors," she says as she runs into the grand hall.

Estrilda stabs it into the huge keyhole and we all work together to heave the great doors open, leaning back and pressing into the floor with our heels.

A sea of people comes rushing towards us now from the grand hall, pushing their way out of the doors. We all quickly take hold of each other again. We do not even manage to squeeze our way out with how furiously everyone is moving—all we can do is keep gripping each other and wait for the rolling waves of people to settle down even by the tiniest margin before we drown.

"Hurry!" the guard cries at everyone, standing to the side and supervising. "Barricade the castle once the doors are shut!" She steps back and swings her arm wildly, and all the guards present rush towards the quickly approaching and enlarging storm of monsters. More and more are coming, and they tear through the guards easily, their forces only slightly slowing the monsters' approaching slaughter.

Alas, with hardly anyone left, the space and fury widen enough for us to go through and we hurry. "Have you seen anyone else?" the guard asks us.

We shake our heads, Sidonie silent and chewing her bottom lip. We'll be the last ones out.

I look beyond the guard. All those who charged at the monsters now lay in a messy line across the hall, the monsters discarding them carelessly. "Barricade the door," she tells us again.

"What about you?" I ask.

"I'll try to buy you all some time."

All us adults nod, fully understanding—perhaps even the children have a sense of what is about to happen. Estrilda pats her cheek as she heads out, Dhea nods a 'thank you', and Hattie smiles tearfully at her as they step outside.

I stop at the doorframe. "What's your name?" Here I go again wasting precious time on that same irrelevant bit of information, but the thing is once you know someone's name, they become a person and I want this woman, who I only ever would have thought of as my enemy and is now something I can't quite define yet, to be a person to me.

"Anice," she says with tears in her eyes.

I nod and reach my foot towards the outside world, towards dirt and air and freedom and space and safety that I haven't known for five years—when Sidonie stays in place, keeping me back.

"Go!" Anice exclaims, tossing her head back and forth between us and the rapidly approaching beasts. My own heart is catapulting as I watch them get closer.

"You can buy us time from out here," Sidonie says firmly.

Anice's eyebrows scrunch together. She shakes her head.

"Sidonie, Marsily!" Maud scolds. "You'll get us all killed! Get out of there!"

Anice looks away from us, and it dawns on me. With all the monsters there are, her staying would hardly be a moment's distraction for them; they'd knock her down without skipping a beat. She knows this. She's not trying to stay for our protection, but for her own. Better to go out in a semblance of glory, a caricature of selflessness, than confront the past five years and all the lives she's contributed to ruining during that time.

But Sidonie won't let her be a hero. And neither will I.

"Come with us," I tell her, and it is an order, not a plea. It is a court sentence, not a rescue effort.

Her lip quivering, she rushes outside with us and we shove the doors shut just as the monsters jump against them.

The gigantic doors shake back and forth, deafening screeches filling the air.

People push us to the side, planting sticks and logs and stones against these doors, and all other doors and windows they come across.

"Step back," I tell Eve and Lili.

"Let's heave that boulder," Estrilda says, pointing to a large one that is as big as Lili and resting unbothered on its own. The other women go around it and push. Even Eve drops my hand to help them.

I glance at Sidonie, who stands hesitantly, tears in her eyes. She gulps harshly and gently lets me go so she may assist in pushing. I take Lili and step aside, wishing I could help but knowing I am in no state to. Others rush to assist them until it is laid securely right against the doors.

Once it is done, they drop their arms and straighten their backs, and we all finally catch our breaths.

"We won the game," Sidonie whispers.

I take a look at our group. Dame Ingrith must have picked us because she thought we were just burdens on everybody else. She put a numerical value on our existences and decided that number wasn't high enough to warrant any extra ounce of patience or effort.

What scale did she even use to measure that? By a rough estimate of years left to live? By how much we can potentially give to others? As if someone needs to be able to contribute something to the world in order to be valuable! As if they're not already worth nurturing simply by virtue of being alive. How wicked is that?

Lili looks down at her feet.

"What's wrong?" I ask her.

"We could have made them our friends," she says.

The lot of us exchange glances, most of us able to keep a blank, nonjudgmental expression except for Maud, who does not mask her raised eyebrows and creased forehead. "Honey," Sidonie attempts to take a poke at this, "I don't think they would want to be our friends."

"They were my mommy's friends. They listened to her."

Could her mother have been the one to lead all of these creatures inside? Could her mother be the cause of all of this?

I have a very bad feeling about her family, and I think she does too. She is still quite young but she has her own wisdom that is only accentuated by her innocence and sweetness.

"She seems like an amazing person," I say. "But not all people are like your mother. Few people can do what she did, and those who can't get hurt."

Anice lets out an audible gasp all of a sudden as she takes Lili in.

"You knew her mother," I realize aloud.

She bites her lip. "It wouldn't have ended like this if she had had her way. There wouldn't have been this bloodshed if she hadn't been—" she stiffens under Lili's stare, whose young eyes are drowning in sorrow yet curiosity "—interrupted."

"Interrupted," Sidonie repeats coldly, making Anice's cheeks flush.

Lili shrinks. Part of her seems to understand, while the other part seems to refuse to. I put my arm around her, holding her from behind in as soft, gentle, and protective of an embrace as I can.

The beginning of a sob stammers out of Anice before she bites it back. She winces, touching her bleeding neck.

Sidonie pulls out a roll of bandage from her pocket. She rips it and holds it up towards Anice. Anice hesitates, her body slumping from shame, but ultimately, she lets Sidonie wrap up her injury.

"I'm sorry," Anice says to all of us, her voice shaking, settling on Lili.

"Don't tell us," Sidnonie says plainly. "Show us."

Anice touches the bandage on her neck, which has effectively stopped the bleeding. A new look falls upon her face, one of determination, one of hope, one of a grasping desire for redemption. She bobs her head at us and then goes into the crowd, helping the lost and traumatized, leading them away from the castle, holding their arms and backs and searching for their loved ones with them.

"Eve!" a voice screeches. We all turn to see a woman guard with blonde hair in disarray bolting towards us. It does not take long for me to remember her as one of the guards who bound and gagged us, her eyebrows pointing sharply at us like the tip of the sword she had directed at our necks. It's funny, how she would have taken part in feeding us to these monsters if these absurd circumstances had not miraculously occurred at the last minute.

"Hi, Auntie Lavender," Eve says softly. The guard bends down and enraptures her small body in her arms, swinging her endearingly from side to side.

"I have something for you," she says, handing her a fuzzy ball the size of her palm. As Eve squeezes it, examining it curiously, Lavender looks up at us. "Have you been taking care of her?"

"We just helped her get out of the castle," I explain.

The relief and gratitude that had captured her entire being now quickly escapes like water out of a hole as she truly takes us all in. Maud is sending her balls of flames with her eyes. Estrilda's jaw is clenched. Dhea stares her down coldly, and Hattie's arms are crossed tightly as she leans against her cane. Even Glinna's brows are furrowed, like she cannot quite place her finger on who this woman is but has an instinctive hatred towards her.

Lavender draws in. She takes Eve's hand and pulls her away hurriedly.

Eve throws her head back at us. "Lili…" she calls.

"You can talk to her later," Lavender mutters, and Lili just waves sadly at her. Helplessly, I do the same, and Sidonie puts a hand on Lili's shoulder.

"Poor child," Hattie mumbles.

"She'll be alright," Dhea says.

We turn to the humongous crowd of survivors, composed of women and men and children and guards.

Estrilda pats my shoulder, smiling at me in accomplishment and disbelief. I hold her fingers in return.

Her eyes move to a spot over my shoulder. She squints and whispers, "Could it be?"

I follow her gaze to an elderly man and three young boys all talking to one another. They each bear a resemblance to Estrilda: one has her nose, another has her wavy hair, the third actually does not have any of her features but vaguely looks like the man. It is this one who catches sight of Estrilda first, gasping and slapping each of the others. Estrilda's mouth drops and she hurries towards who must be her husband and grandkids. Simultaneously, they all rush towards her as fast as they can, the boys almost knocking her over.

We all beam at this.

"None of us ever imagined her reuniting with them again in this life," Dhea says brightly.

She and Hattie exchange whispers between them, and then Hattie speaks up. "Dhea and I are going to search for anyone we know as well."

"We do not have high hopes but we have hope nonetheless," Dhea adds.

"This is where we shall part ways as well," Maud says.

Dhea and Hattie hug each of us. Hattie picks up her cane to wrap me up in her hug, and Dhea squeezes tight enough with one arm to act as two. I wince as she accidentally hits my torn arm, sending reverberations of pain through it. She cringes. "I beg your pardon." I pat her in a 'no harm done' way (even if that is not quite true).

Glinna also throws her arms around us—with Maud just hanging in the back— pleasantly surprising me, and I warmly accept it.

Rubbing my shoulder, I glance at each of them, hoping to sear each of them into my memory forever, just in case. "We would not have made it without each one of you," I tell them.

They smile and disappear into the crazy swarm of lost but rejuvenated people.

Maud starts to go without a word, when she abruptly stops and turns. "Marsily. Sidonie," she says. "Thank you." Then, she too leaves with Glinna.

Sidonie takes my and Lili's hands, leading us a bit away from the crowd, not wandering too far but just far enough that we can breathe.

I glance back at the castle. It seems fairly locked up now, but I can't help but wonder if the monsters will be able to find a way out eventually. I wonder if Lili has a point, that we will need to learn to coexist with them in the future. I wonder if we will be capable of doing so.

Sidonie gestures to a spot on the ground and we sit around. She empties out all the contents in her pockets, spreading the vials and wrapped pastries around the space between the three of us. She pushes the pastries towards Lili. "Have the rest."

Lili timidly reaches for one. "You can have some, too," she says.

"That's kind of you," Sidonie says appreciatively. She picks up the medicine bottles. "Don't look, alright?"

Lili turns around as she chews the muffin. Sidonie unwraps the strip tied around my arm, and even I cannot bear to look at what is beneath it. Then, she pours medicines into it, dabbing at it and working on it. All I can do is sharply inhale and clench my hands, grabbing fistfuls of dirt that jam beneath my fingernails, goosebumps appearing all over and my spine shuddering. Sidonie kisses the top of my head and wraps the wound up again.

When I turn back to her, her dress is even shorter now and her eyes are filled with tears. I lean against her, sighing heavily, tapping Lili on the shoulder and inviting her in as well.

"Well, I'll be damned," a deep, manly voice says from bchind us.

We look up and it is a tall, portly man. It takes me a moment, and then memories from what feel like another life rush into me. The man is Sidonie's uncle! The same one who welcomed me into his home every time he caught sight of me and made sure to have Sidonie pass along that message every time he didn't.

Next to him is a bright-eyed woman with braids identical to Sidonie's—Amira, Sidonie's cousin!

Sidonie rushes to her feet and jumps into both of their arms, bursting into tears. "I thought you were dead!"

"We escaped through a window before everything was sealed up," Amira cries into her.

"And you, Uncle Allard," Sidonie blubbers. "I can't believe…" She leaves the sentence hanging in the air as tears take over.

"Goodness, you and Amira have both grown so much," he whispers gingerly.

"As have you," Sidonie says.

Indeed, his curly black hair and mustache have traces of grey in them. "Hush, don't say that," he says. The three of them laugh through tears.

I smile, my heart both light and heavy all at once. Lili slips her little hand into mine, this small gesture enough to make me melt inside. I squeeze her hand gently, in an act of comfort and promise of nurturing.

Sidonie, Amira, and Allard release one another. Amira looks at my arm and slowly hugs me, extremely careful not to jostle it even by the tiniest inch. "It's really good to see you," I tell her.

Allard bends down to hug me as well. "That's another face I never thought I'd see again," he says, chuckling heartily. As they sit down beside us, introducing themselves to Lili, I still cannot believe any of this is actually happening. It would still make more sense for all of this to be another product of my unreliable mind.

As the intensity and insanity of everything finally starts to wear down, a few people trickle away but almost everyone stays in place, surrounding the general area outside the castle. I notice people glancing at each other, fearful and confused. Even the guards are at a loss of what to do, seemingly not even sure if they should try to reclaim authority. We can all feel the power vortex sitting in the air, just waiting for someone to claim it.

I get closer to the general crowd and climb on top of an empty stone bench draped with dirt. "Everyone," I say loudly, a few people turning away from their own conversations to look at me.

Sidonie climbs up next to me. "EVERYONE!" she booms, snatching everyone's attention.

"We should go into the city and scour for supplies! Tend to the wounded!" I shout, doing my best to make it reach as many people as possible, my throat quickly getting sore.

"Things cannot run the same way they have been for years and years!" Sidonie adds sternly, glaring at each knight she can spot. "We've been forced together, and now we must stay together if we hope to make it out here!"

There are shouts of agreement, fervent nods, and fists thrown passionately in the air. Villagers step towards us, several guards hesitantly dropping their weapons and doing the same.

"You madwoman!" I hear some shouts, and I spot several people scattered about that shake their head and curl their lips at us with disbelief at our absurdity.

A couple men lift a woman up on their shoulders, making her head peak above the crowd. "If you believe we will ever cooperate with those tyrants again, you are sadly mistaken!" she yells, jabbing her finger at the guards. "And there is no way I am staying anywhere near those creatures!"

"Let's leave Orienne!" one of the men holding her yells, and a flurry of cheers follow.

"Where would you go?" Sidonie shouts back.

"We found this!" the woman answers. One of the men is holding a ragged, badly sown together sack. He pulls a creased piece of paper out and hands it to her, and she holds it open for all to see, revealing a map. "We'll let it guide us on the long journey to a whole new land. Those who agree, follow me!"

The crowd slowly splits into two, half of them encircling that woman, the other half ebbing around us.

Sidonie and I jump down to the ground.

"Perhaps the smartest move *is* to leave Orienne," Allard says.

"Perhaps," Sidonie says, "but I know most of us require some time before we can even start to formulate the logistics of such a plan."

"We can start off by scouring the houses here up to the square," one man says to us, a small group behind him seeming to echo his sentiment.

Sidonie nods. "That would be wonderful."

I watch the scene before me, realizing that this is the entire kingdom of Orienne. Everyone is out here—out of the castle, and out of everything our lives used to be.

Many people move about, while others stay in place as they converse and figure themselves out. But no matter what everyone is doing, they are all doing something.

Suddenly, it feels like I am drowning all over again with how overwhelming everything is and is about to be.

I don't understand fate and the way the world works. Why people are the way they are. Why life is the way it is. Why some people get more than what they deserve, while some get none of it.

All I know is that I am alive—me and all the people here.

And my goodness do I want a happy ending.

I look at Sidonie and Lili and Amira and Allard. I look at myself.

I realize the freedom we now have. The price that was paid to get here. I hope we can take this opportunity and grow something beautiful out of it, craft a garden for the future out of the weeds that we escaped from. At the very least, I hope we can make it worth it. That we can make it something *good*, if not permanently, then at least for as long as possible.

We are all here living in the shadows of the lives, legacies, and sacrifices of those before us. We have to do what we can with the time we have, and trust that by the time it runs out, those after us will do the same. Then maybe eventually, the traces of their lives will make it back to us, wherever we will be.

I hug them all again with my good arm.

Sidonie smiles and sighs; fear, uncertainty, hope, and determination clear in that release of air. "Orienne," she says, "here we come."